Larry Delaney:

Lonesome Genius

by

Frank O'Connor

Killeen Books
Killeen,
Blackrock Village,
Cork City,
Republic of Ireland.

The texts used in this edition are taken from the *Stories of Frank O'Connor*,
Hamish Hamilton 1953, *Domestic Relations*, Hamish Hamilton 1957 reproduced
by kind permission of Penguin UK and from *Guests of The Nation* Macmillan
1931 reproduced by kind permission of Peters, Fraser & Dunlop Group Ltd.

This selection first published by Killeen Books 1996
1 3 5 6 4 2

ISBN 1 873548 35 4

Cover Photograph: Boy Catching Mackerel, Youghal 1949
reproduced by kind permission of Tom Cotter
©Tom Cotter 1996

Typeset by the publishers in Adobe Garamond 11.5 pt

Printed in Dublin by Colour Books
on acid free paper

Contents

INTRODUCTION

Frank O'Connor, in his writings, showed how the Irish Free State failed to treat all her children equally, how her revolution was a sham. Yet these political revelations were by-products of his artistic aims. He was not a politically-motivated social-realist. Form was O'Connor's main motivator. O'Connor had a very definite idea of what did and did not constitute a short story, it was not a slice of life, it was not just a fiction of a certain length.

O'Connor has often been criticised for being too traditional. How can one be too traditional in an art form that is less than a hundred years old? Writers like O'Connor and Isaac Bashevis Singer fashioned the tradition. To castigate O'Connor for not writing 'experimental short-stories' is like castigating a Shakespearean sonnet specialist for not writing free verse! All sonnets may be poems but not all poems are sonnets. All short stories may be short fictions but not all short fictions are short stories. Whether a writer concentrates on a certain form or not is nobody's business but his own. The real question is how successful was the writer in his chosen form?

O'Connor was obsessive about 'getting it right'. Whenever an occasion demanded a new appearance for an old story he would scrutinise every clause for room for improvement and if necessary rewrite without scruples. O'Faolain, referred to this revising as a form of forgery. But visual artists, such as Le Brocquy, keep reworking the same material in an effort to reach perfection — why shouldn't a writer?

How do we judge that O'Connor was successful in his chosen form? We could point to the sales of his books — extraordinary for short stories. We could note the frequent acknowledgments to *The New Yorker*— the most prestigious outlet for short stories in the world. We could note how O'Connor, a man whom the Christian Brothers encouraged to leave school at fourteen, was invited to lecture in Harvard and Trinity on the subject of the short story. Or we could take stories like 'The Procession of Life', which O'Connor wrote over sixty years ago, and see how fresh and provocative they still are. Who as the century closes can read Robert Coover's avant garde *Pricksongs And Descants*? After just thirty years this primary achievement of American experimental short fiction is unreadable!

It might have sounded like self-praise but when O'Connor declared the following he was merely stating what can now be read as the plain truth:

'I know that there is only one correct way to write a story, and that is the way I do it. If there were a more correct way, I'd use that. That doesn't mean that I'm blind to the merits of other writers. On the contrary, considering that they use the wrong methods, I think it is remarkable that they should write as well as they do. But I think they would write still better if they wrote in my way.'

There is humour in that statement like there is humour in almost everything O'Connor wrote. But the humour does not detract from the seriousness of what is being said.

In the following stories we laugh at Larry Delaney and if we are lazy readers we might well miss how really terrible his life is. But O'Connor never missed it — because he lived it. Nobody better than O'Connor knew what it was like to live in an Irish working-class slum and nobody was better equipped to think deeply about it. But while the protagonists of Doyle and Bolger might turn to Rock and Drugs for comfort, Larry Delaney's people had a choice of only the boat, the drink or laughter. Frank O'Connor witnessed his father and others on drink and chose laughter.

No Irish writer has suffered greater for his laughter. In recent times O'Connor has been compared disfavourably with the likes of Samuel Beckett. Beckett was from a privileged middle-class family. He attended good schools and graduated from

Trinity College. Beckett never had to justify holding a book in his hand as Larry Delaney must do, again and again. In his formative years Beckett never had to worry where the next meal should come from. Beckett as a writer was forced by aesthetic necessity to internalise, to write novels and fictions whose form derived from rumination and contemplation. Beckett as a young writer could never construct conventional external dramas because his life was free of them. All of Beckett's crises are in his head; that fact does not make him the better writer, only a different one. Both Beckett and O'Connor wrote obsessively about their mothers and we as readers are enriched by having two such diverse treatments. Contemporary working-class Irish writers are able to benefit from both aesthetic paths when coming to write their own work. Borges showed us how Kafka drew on mutually incompatible writers as precursors and that is what is happening today in the work of Dermot Bolger and Roddy Doyle. Both show Beckett and O'Connor as prominent precursors along with a number of other writers. No Irish fiction writer at the end of the millennium is free of Joyce's influence but Flann O'Brien, Brendan Behan, Sean O'Casey and less frequently Francis Stuart also figure in the works of Doyle and Bolger. Other writers look to Elizabeth Bowen, Kate O'Brien and Mary Lavin for succour.

But nobody can discuss the work of Bolger and Doyle, the two most influential, contemporary, working-class authors, without reference to O'Connor. Roddy Doyle in particular displays the influence of O'Connor through his reliance on dialogue. And even when he is not relying on dialogue, as in his most recent work, the plausible voice of an individual narrator is ever present. O'Connor called his seminal study of the short story *The Lonely Voice* because he believed that the short story form was dependent on the presence of an individual voice. Nowadays Doyle is writing whole novels sustained by that lonely voice.

Francis Stuart once accused Frank O'Connor of being the soft-centre of Irish Writing, in so doing Stuart acted as nurse-maid to a whole asylum of soft-headed Irish literary critics, incapable of discerning any worth in texts devoid of stylistic and socio-philosophical pretensions.

Stuart, using the opening paragraph of 'A First Confession' as his only evidence, accused O'Connor of being a toady to the Irish state, of fulfilling a function analogous to that served by the Soviet Writers' Union to the Socialist Republics.

O'Connor's work treated the struggles of a submerged population who never had a literature to call their own, an urban and rural working class whose sons and daughters were forced abroad not out of bourgeois ennui like Stuart, but by the basic need for physical sustenance.

While Francis Stuart co-existed with the consensus prevailing in Hitler's Mitteleuropa, (justifying his presence there by recourse to some anti-bourgeois aesthetic) free to earn a comfortable living as a university lecturer and Reichesradio broadcaster, Frank O'Connor, his wife and children faced penury in a state which actively prevented him from making a living as a writer and broadcaster — because he dared to criticise the absurdities of Cosgrave's and De Valera's delusions and Fascist ignominy. Frank O'Connor was anything but an apologist for the Irish Free State.

It is easy to understand why Francis Stuart, a one-time black-listed writer, should resent the best-selling, world-renowned Frank O'Connor. It is more puzzling that Stuart's mean-spirited, misreadings of O'Connor should be embraced by sections of the Irish intelligentsia.

Just as the socially-aspiring Larry Delaney is constantly em-barrassed by his father's incorrigible working-class traits. O'Connor's non-pretentious, accessible short stories written in an authentic but unsophisticated Irish voice are hated by metropolitan professionals who would seek to deny anything

Irish not derivative of mainstream European culture. In the words of Delaney's father 'they're better fed than taught!' Declan Kiberd in his recently published literary history of Ireland has invented an Ireland in which O'Connor barely receives a mention. In contrast Richard Forde, in his short introduction to the Granta book of *American* Short Stories, refers to O'Connor no less than seven times. There are Irish critics who would celebrate the regional authenticity and originality of a Bruno Schulz , but when it comes to their own authentic writers they spurn them in a pathetic provincial lack of self-awareness. In literary politics Dublin is the most provincial of world capitals. In Dublin like so many of our unskilled emigrants, Frank O'Connor is an embarrassment to the establishment — on the world stage he is still a giant.

Patrick Cotter
June 1996

The Idealist

I don't know how it is about education, but it never seemed to do anything for me but get me into trouble.

Adventure stories weren't so bad, but as a kid I was very serious and preferred realism to romance. School stories were what I liked best, and, judged by our standards, these were romantic enough for anyone. The schools were English, so I suppose you couldn't expect anything else. They were always called 'the venerable pile', and there was usually a ghost in them; they were built in a square that was called 'the quad', and, according to the pictures, they were all clock-towers, spires, and pinnacles, like the lunatic asylum with us. The fellows in the stories were all good climbers, and got in and out of school at night on ropes made of knotted sheets. They dressed queerly; they wore long trousers, short, black jackets, and top hats. Whenever they did anything wrong they were given 'lines' in Latin. When it was a bad case, they were flogged and never showed any sign of pain; only the bad fellows, and they always said: 'Ow! Ow!'

Most of them were grand chaps who always stuck together and were great at football and cricket. They never told lies and wouldn't talk to anyone who did. If they were caught out and asked a point-blank question, they always told the truth, unless someone else was with them, and then even if they were to be expelled for it they wouldn't give his name, even if he was a thief, which, as a matter of fact, he frequently was. It was surprising in such good schools, with fathers who never gave less than five quid, the numbers of thieves there were. The fellows in our school hardly ever stole, though they only got a penny a week, and sometimes not even that, as when their fathers were on the booze and their mothers had to go to the pawn.

I worked hard at the football and cricket, though of course we never had a proper football and the cricket we played was with a hurley stick against a wicket chalked on some wall. The officers in the barrack played proper cricket, and on summer evenings I used to go and watch them, like one of the souls in Purgatory watching the joys of Paradise.

Even so, I couldn't help being disgusted at the bad way things were run in our school. Our 'venerable pile' was a redbrick building without tower or pinnacle a fellow could climb, and no ghost at all: we had no team, so a fellow, no matter how hard he worked, could never play for the school, and, instead of giving you 'lines', Latin or any other sort, Murderer Moloney either lifted you by the ears or bashed you with a cane. When he got tired of bashing you on the hands he bashed you on the legs.

But these were only superficial things. What was really wrong was ourselves. The fellows sucked up to the masters and told them all that went on. If they were caught out in anything they tried to put the blame on someone else, even if it meant telling lies. When they were caned they snivelled and said it wasn't fair; drew back their hands as if they were terrified, so that the cane caught only the tips of their fingers and then screamed and stood on one leg, shaking out their fingers in the hope of getting it counted as one. Finally they roared that their wrist was broken and crawled back to their desks with their hands squeezed under their armpits, howling. I mean you couldn't help feeling ashamed, imagining what chaps from a decent school would think if they saw it.

My own way to school led me past the barrack gate. In those peaceful days sentries never minded you going past the guard-room to have a look at the chaps drilling in the barrack square; if you came at dinnertime they even called you in and gave you plumduff and tea. Naturally, with such temptations I was often late. The only excuse, short of a letter from your mother, was to say you were at early Mass. The Murderer would never know whether you were or not, and if he did anything to you, you could easily get him into trouble with the parish priest. Even as kids we knew who the real boss of the school was.

But after I started reading those confounded school stories I was never happy about saying I had been to Mass. It was a lie, and I knew that the chaps in the stories would have died sooner than tell it. They were all round me like invisible presences, and I hated to do anything which I felt they might disapprove of. One morning I came in very late and rather frightened.

'What kept you till this hour, Delaney?' Murderer Moloney asked, looking at the clock.

I wanted to say I had been at Mass, but I couldn't. The invisible presences were all about me.

'I was delayed at the barrack, sir,' I replied in panic.

There was a faint titter from the class, and Moloney raised his brows in mild surprise. He was a big powerful man with fair hair and blue eyes and a manner that at times was deceptively mild.

'Oh, indeed,' he said, politely enough. 'And what delayed you?'

'I was watching the soldiers drilling, sir,' I said.

The class tittered again. This was a new line entirely for them.

'Oh,' Moloney said casually, 'I never knew you were such a military man. Hold out your hand!'

Compared with the laughter the slaps were nothing, and besides, I had the example of the invisible presences to sustain me. I did not flinch. I returned to my desk slowly and quietly without snivelling or squeezing my hands, and the Murderer looked after me, raising his brows again as though to indicate that this was a new line for him, too. But the others gaped and whispered as if I were some strange animal. At playtime they gathered about me, full of curiosity and excitement.

'Delaney, why did you say that about the barrack?'

'Because 'twas true,' I replied firmly. 'I wasn't going to tell him a lie.'

'What lie?'

'That I was at Mass.'

'Then couldn't you say you had to go on a message?'

'That would be a lie too.'

'Cripes, Delaney,' they said, 'you'd better mind yourself. The Murderer is in an awful wax. He'll massacre you.'

I knew that. I knew only too well that the Murderer's professional pride had been deeply wounded, and for the rest of the day I was on my best behaviour. But my best wasn't enough, for I underrated the Murderer's guile. Though he pretended to be reading, he was watching me the whole time.

'Delaney,' he said at last without raising his head from the book, 'was that you talking?'

''Twas, sir,' I replied in consternation.

The whole class laughed. They couldn't believe but that I was deliberately trailing my coat, and, of course, the laugh must have convinced him that I was. I suppose if people do tell you lies all day and every day, it soon becomes a sort of perquisite which you resent being deprived of.

'Oh,' he said, throwing down his book, 'we'll soon stop that.'

This time it was a tougher job, because he was really on his mettle. But so was I. I knew this was the testing-point for me, and if only I could keep my head I should provide a model for the whole class. When I had got through the ordeal without moving a muscle, and returned to my desk with my hands by my sides, the invisible presences gave me a great clap. But the visible ones were nearly as annoyed as the Murderer himself. After school half a dozen of them followed me down the school yard.

'Go on!' they shouted truculently. 'Shaping as usual!'

'I was not shaping.'

'You were shaping. You're always showing off. Trying to pretend he didn't hurt you a blooming crybaby like you!'

'I wasn't trying to pretend,' I shouted, even then resisting the temptation to nurse my bruised hands. 'Only decent fellows don't cry over every little pain like kids.'

'Go on!' they bawled after me. 'You ould idiot!'

And, as I went down the school lane, still trying to keep what the stories called 'a stiff upper lip', and consoling myself with the thought that my torment was over until next morning, I heard their mocking voices after me. 'Loony Larry! Yah, Loony Larry!'

I realised that if I was to keep on terms with the invisible presences I should have to watch my step at school.

So I did, all through that year. But one day an awful thing happened. I was coming in from the yard, and in the porch outside our schoolroom I saw a fellow called Gorman taking something from a coat on the rack. I always described Gorman to myself as 'the black sheep of the school'. He was a fellow I disliked and feared; a handsome, sulky spoiled, and sneering lout. I paid no attention to him because I had escaped for a few moments into my dream-world in which fathers never gave less than fivers and the honour of the school was always saved by some quiet, unassuming fellow like myself 'a dark horse', as the stories called him.

'Who are you looking at?' Gorman asked threateningly.

'I wasn't looking at anyone,' I replied with an indignant start.

'I was only getting a pencil out of my coat,' he added, clenching his fists.

'Nobody said you weren't,' I replied, thinking that this was a very queer subject to start a row about.

'You'd better not, either,' he snarled. 'You can mind your own business.'

'You mind yours!' I retorted, purely for the purpose of saving face. 'I never spoke to you at all.'

And that, so far as I was concerned, was the end of it.

But after playtime the Murderer, looking exceptionally serious, stood before the class, balancing a pencil in both hands.

'Everyone who left the classroom this morning, stand out!' he called. Then he lowered his head and looked at us from under his brows. 'Mind now, I said everyone!'

I stood out with the others, including Gorman. We were all very puzzled.

'Did you take anything from a coat on the rack this morning?' the Murderer asked, laying a heavy, hairy paw on Gorman's shoulder and staring menacingly into his eyes.

'Me, sir?' Gorman exclaimed innocently. 'No, sir.'

'Did you see anyone else doing it?' 'No, sir.'

'You?' he asked another lad, but even before he reached me at all I realised why Gorman had told the lie and wondered frantically what I should do.

'You?' he asked me, and his big red face was close to mine, his blue eyes were only a few inches away, and the smell of his toilet soap was in my nostrils. My panic made me say the wrong thing as though I had planned it.

'I didn't take anything, sir,' I said in a low voice.

'Did you see someone else do it?' he asked, raising his brows and showing quite plainly that he had noticed my evasion. 'Have you a tongue in your head?' he shouted suddenly, and the whole class, electrified, stared at me. 'You?' he added curtly to the next boy as though he had lost interest in me.

'No, sir.'

'Back to your desks, the rest of you!' he ordered. 'Delaney, you stay here.'

He waited till everyone was seated again before going on.

'Turn out your pockets.'

I did, and a half-stifled giggle rose, which the Murderer quelled with a thunderous glance. Even for a small boy I had pockets that were museums in themselves: the purpose of half the things I brought to light I couldn't have explained myself. They were antiques, prehistoric and unlabelled. Among them was a school story borrowed the previous evening from a queer fellow who chewed paper as if it were gum. The Murderer reached out for it, and holding it at arm's length, shook it out with an expression of deepening disgust as he noticed the nibbled corners and margins.

'Oh,' he said disdainfully, 'so this is how you waste your time! What do you do with this rubbish eat it?'

''Tisn't mine, sir,' I said against the laugh that sprang up. 'I borrowed it.'

'Is that what you did with the money?' he asked quickly, his fat head on one side.

'Money?' I repeated in confusion. 'What money?'

'The shilling that was stolen from Flanagan's overcoat this morning. (Flanagan was a little hunchback whose people coddled him; no one else in the school would have possessed that much money.)

'I never took Flanagan's shilling,' I said, beginning to cry, 'and you have no right to say I did.'

'I have the right to say you're the most impudent and defiant puppy in the school,' he replied, his voice hoarse with rage, 'and I wouldn't put it past you. What else can anyone expect and you reading this dirty, rotten, filthy rubbish?' And he tore my school story in halves and flung them to the farthest corner of the classroom. 'Dirty, filthy, English rubbish! Now, hold out your hand.'

This time the invisible presences deserted me. Hearing themselves described in these contemptuous terms, they fled. The Murderer went mad in the way people do whenever they're up against something they don't understand. Even the other fellows were shocked, and, heaven knows, they had little sympathy with me.

'You should put the police on him,' they advised me later in the playground.

'He lifted the cane over his shoulder. He could get the jail for that.'

'But why didn't you say you didn't see anyone?' asked the eldest, a fellow called Spillane.

'Because I did,' I said, beginning to sob all over again at the memory of my wrongs. 'I saw Gorman.'

'Gorman?' Spillane echoed incredulously. 'Was it Gorman took Flanagan's money? And why didn't you say so?'

'Because it wouldn't be right,' I sobbed.

'Why wouldn't it be right?'

'Because Gorman should have told the truth himself,' I said. 'And if this was a proper school he'd be sent to Coventry.'

'He'd be sent where?'

'Coventry. No one would ever speak to him again.'

'But why would Gorman tell the truth if he took the money?' Spillane asked as you'd speak to a baby. 'Jay, Delaney,' he added pityingly, 'you're getting madder and madder. Now, look at what you're after bringing on yourself!'

Suddenly Gorman came lumbering up, red and angry.

'Delaney,' he shouted threateningly, 'did you say I took Flanagan's money?' Gorman, though I of course didn't realise it, was as much at sea as Moloney and the rest. Seeing me take all that punishment rather than give him away, he concluded that I must be more afraid of him than of Moloney, and that the proper thing to do was to make me more so. He couldn't have come at a time when I cared less for him. I didn't even bother to reply but lashed out with all my strength at his brutal face. This was the last thing he expected. He screamed, and his hand came away from his face, all blood. Then he threw off his satchel and came at me, but at the same moment a door opened behind us and a lame teacher called Murphy emerged. We all ran like mad and the fight was forgotten.

It didn't remain forgotten, though. Next morning after prayers the Murderer scowled at me.

'Delaney, were you fighting in the yard after school yesterday?' For a second or two I didn't reply. I couldn't help feeling that it wasn't worth it. But before the invisible presences fled for ever, I made another effort.

'I was, sir,' I said, and this time there wasn't even a titter. I was out of my mind. The whole class knew it and was awe-stricken.

'Who were you fighting?'

'I'd sooner not say, sir,' I replied, hysteria beginning to well up in me. It was all very well for the invisible presences, but they hadn't to deal with the Murderer.

'Who was he fighting with?' he asked lightly, resting his hands on the desk and studying the ceiling.

'Gorman, sir,' replied three or four voices as easy as that!

'Did Gorman hit him first?'

'No, sir. He hit Gorman first.'

'Stand out,' he said, taking up the cane. 'Now,' he added, going up to Gorman, 'you take this and hit him. And make sure you hit him hard,' he went on, giving Gorman's arm an encouraging squeeze. 'He thinks he's a great fellow. You show him now what we think of him.'

Gorman came towards me with a broad grin. He thought it a great joke. The class thought it a great joke. They began to roar with laughter. Even the Murderer permitted himself a modest grin at his own cleverness.

'Hold out your hand,' he said to me.

I didn't. I began to feel trapped and a little crazy.

'Hold out your hand, I say,' he shouted, beginning to lose his temper.

'I will not,' I shouted back, losing all control of myself.

'You what?' he cried incredulously, dashing at me round the classroom with his hand raised as though to strike me. 'What's that you said, you dirty little thief?'

'I'm not a thief, I'm not a thief,' I screamed. 'And if he comes near me I'll kick the shins off him. You have no right to give him that cane, and you have no right to call me a thief either. If you do it again, I'll go down to the police and then we'll see who the thief is.'

'You refused to answer my questions,' he roared, and if I had been in my right mind I should have known he had suddenly taken fright; probably the word 'police' had frightened him.

'No,' I said through my sobs, 'and I won't answer them now either. I'm not a spy.'

'Oh,' he retorted with a sarcastic sniff, 'so that's what you call a spy, Mr Delaney?'

'Yes, and that's what they all are, all the fellows here dirty spies! But I'm not going to spy for you. You can do your own spying.'

'That's enough now, that's enough!' he said, raising his fat hand almost beseechingly. 'There's no need to lose control of yourself, my dear young fellow, and there's no need whatever to screech like that. 'Tis most unmanly. Go back to your seat now and I'll talk to you another time.'

I obeyed, but I did no work. No one else did much either. The hysteria had spread to the class. I alternated between fits of exultation at my own successful defiance of the Murderer, and panic at the prospect of his revenge; and at each change of mood I put my face in my hands and sobbed again. The Murderer didn't even order me to stop. He didn't so much as look at me.

After that I was the hero of the school for the whole afternoon. Gorman tried to resume the fight, but Spillane ordered him away contemptuously a fellow who had taken the master's cane to another had no status. But that wasn't the sort of hero I wanted to be. I preferred something less sensational.

Next morning I was in such a state of panic that I didn't know how I should face school at all. I dawdled, between two minds as to whether or not I should mitch. The silence of the school lane and yard awed me. I had made myself late as well.

'What kept you, Delaney?' the Murderer asked quietly.

I knew it was no good.

'I was at Mass, sir.'

'All right. Take your seat.'

He seemed a bit surprised. What I had not realised was the incidental advantage of our system over the English one. By this time half a dozen of his pets had brought the Murderer the true story of Flanagan's shilling, and if he didn't feel a monster he probably felt a fool.

But by that time I didn't care. In my school sack I had another story. Not a school story this time, though. School stories were a washout. 'Bang! Bang!' that was the only way to deal with men like the Murderer. 'The only good teacher is a dead teacher.'

My Oedipus Complex

Father was in the army all through the war the First War, I mean so, up to the age of five, I never saw much of him, and what I saw did not worry me. Sometimes I woke and there was a big figure in khaki peering down at me in the candlelight. Sometimes in the early morning I heard the slamming of the front door and the clatter of nailed boots down the cobbles of the lane. These were Father's entrances and exits. Like Santa Claus he came and went mysteriously.

In fact, I rather liked his visits, though it was an uncomfortable squeeze between Mother and him when I got into the big bed in the early morning. He smoked, which gave him a pleasant musty smell, and shaved, an operation of astounding interest. Each time he left a trail of souvenirs model tanks and Gurkha knives with handles made of bullet cases, and German helmets and cap badges and button-sticks, and all sorts of military equipment carefully stowed away in a long box on top of the wardrobe, in case they ever came in handy. There was a bit of the magpie about Father; he expected everything to come in handy. When his back was turned, Mother let me get a chair and rummage through his treasures. She didn't seem to think so highly of them as he did. The war was the most peaceful period of my life. The window of my attic faced south-east. My Mother had curtained it, but that had small effect. I always woke with the first light and, with all the responsibilities of the previous day melted, feeling myself rather like the sun, ready to illumine and rejoice. Life never seemed so simple and clear and full of possibilities as then. I put my feet out from under the clothes I called them Mrs Left and Mrs Right and invented dramatic situations for them in which they discussed the problems of the day. At least Mrs Right did; she was very demonstrative, but I hadn't the same control of Mrs Left, so she mostly contented herself with nodding agreement.

They discussed what Mother and I should do during the day, what Santa Claus should give a fellow for Christmas, and what steps should be taken to brighten the home. There was that little matter of the baby, for instance. Mother and I could never agree about that. Ours was the only house in the terrace without a new baby, and Mother said we couldn't afford one till Father came back from the war because they cost seventeen and six. That showed how simple she was. The Geneys up the road had a baby, and everyone knew they couldn't afford seventeen and six. It was probably a cheap baby, and Mother wanted something really good, but I felt she was too exclusive. The Geneys' baby would have done us fine.

Having settled my plans for the day, I got up, put a chair under the attic window, and lifted the frame high enough to stick out my head. The window overlooked the front gardens of the terrace behind ours, and beyond these it looked over a deep valley to the tall, red-brick houses terraced up the opposite hillside, which were all still in shadow, while those at our side of the valley were all lit up, though with long strange shadows that made them seem unfamiliar; rigid and painted.

After that I went into Mother's room and climbed into the big bed. She woke and I began to tell her of my schemes. By this time, though I never seem to have noticed it, I was petrified in my nightshirt, and I thawed as I talked until, the last frost melted, I fell asleep beside her and woke again only when I heard her below in the kitchen, making the breakfast.

After breakfast we went into town; heard Mass at St Augustine's and said a prayer for Father, and did the shopping. If the afternoon was fine we either went for a walk in the country or a visit to Mother's great friend in the convent, Mother St Dominic. Mother had them all praying for Father, and every night, going to bed, I asked God to send him back safe from the war to us. Little, indeed, did I know what I was praying for!

One morning I got into the big bed, and there, sure enough, was Father in his usual Santa Claus manner but later, instead of uniform, he put on his best blue suit, and Mother was as pleased as anything. I saw nothing to be pleased about, because, out of uniform, Father was altogether less interesting, but she only beamed, and explained that our prayers had been answered, and off we went to Mass to thank God for having brought Father safely home.

The irony of it! That very day when he came in to dinner he took off his boots and put on his slippers, donned the dirty old cap he wore about the house to save him from colds, crossed his legs, and began to talk gravely to Mother, who looked anxious. Naturally, I disliked her looking anxious, because it destroyed her good looks, so I interrupted him.

'Just a moment, Larry!' she said gently.

This was only what she said when we had boring visitors, so I attached no importance to it and went on talking.

'Do be quiet, Larry!' she said impatiently. 'Don't you hear me talking to Daddy?'

This was the first time I had heard those ominous words, 'talking to Daddy', and I couldn't help feeling that if this was how God answered prayers, he couldn't listen to them very attentively.

'Why are you talking to Daddy?' I asked with as great a show of indifference as I could muster.

'Because Daddy and I have business to discuss. Now don't interrupt again!'

In the afternoon, at Mother's request, Father took me for a walk. This time we went into town instead of out to the country, and I thought at first, in my usual optimistic way, that it might be an improvement. It was nothing of the sort. Father and I had quite different notions of a walk in town. He had no proper interest in trams, ships, and horses, and the only thing that seemed to divert him was talking to fellows as old as himself. When I wanted to stop he simply went on, dragging me behind him by the hand; when he wanted to stop I had no alternative but to do the same. I noticed that it seemed to be a sign that he wanted to stop for a long time whenever he leaned against a wall. The second time I saw him do it I got wild. He seemed to be settling himself forever. I pulled him by the coat and trousers, but, unlike Mother who, if you were too persistent, got into a wax and said: 'Larry, if you don't behave yourself, I'll give you a good slap,' Father had an extraordinary capacity for amiable inattention. I sized him up and wondered would I cry, but he seemed to be too remote to be annoyed even by that. Really, it was like going for a walk with a mountain! He either ignored the wrenching and pummeling entirely, or else glanced down with a grin of amusement from his peak. I had never met anyone so absorbed in himself as he seemed.

At teatime, 'talking to Daddy' began again, complicated this time by the fact that he had an evening paper, and every few minutes he put it down and told Mother something new out of it. I felt this was foul play. Man for man, I was prepared to compete with him any time for Mother's attention, but when he had it all made up for him by other people it left me no chance. Several times I tried to change the subject without success.

'You must be quiet while Daddy is reading, Larry,' Mother said impatiently.

It was clear that she either genuinely liked talking to Father better than talking to me, or else that he had some terrible hold on her which made her afraid to admit the truth.

'Mummy,' I said that night when she was tucking me up, 'do you think if I prayed hard God would send Daddy back to the war?' She seemed to think about that for a moment.

'No, dear,' she said with a smile. 'I don't think he would.'

'Why wouldn't he, Mummy?'

'Because there isn't a war any longer, dear.'

'But, Mummy, couldn't God make another war, if He liked?'

'He wouldn't like to, dear. It's not God who makes wars, but bad people.'

'Oh!' I said.

I was disappointed about that. I began to think that God wasn't quite what he was cracked up to be.

Next morning I woke at my usual hour, feeling like a bottle of champagne. I put out my feet and invented a long conversation in which Mrs Right talked of the trouble she had with her own father till she put him in the Home. I didn't quite know what the Home was but it sounded the right place for Father. Then I got my chair and stuck my head out of the attic window. Dawn was just breaking, with a guilty air that made me feel I had caught it in the act. My head bursting with stories and schemes, I stumbled in next door, and in the half-darkness scrambled into the big bed. There was no room at Mother's side so I had to get between her and Father. For the time being I had forgotten about him, and for several minutes I sat bolt upright, racking my brains to know what I could do with him. He was taking up more than his fair share of the bed, and I couldn't get comfortable, so I gave him several kicks that made him grunt and stretch. He made room all right, though. Mother waked and felt for me. I settled back comfortably in the warmth of the bed with my thumb in my mouth. 'Mummy!' I hummed, loudly and contentedly.

'Sssh! dear,' she whispered. 'Don't wake Daddy!'

This was a new development, which threatened to be even more serious than 'talking to Daddy'. Life without my early morning conferences was unthinkable.

'Why?' I asked severely.

'Because poor Daddy is tired.'

This seemed to me a quite inadequate reason, and I was sickened by the sentimentality of her 'poor Daddy'. I never liked that sort of gush; it always struck me as insincere.

'Oh!' I said lightly. Then in my most winning tone: 'Do you know where I want to go with you today, Mummy?'

'No, dear,' she sighed.

'I want to go down the Glen and fish for thornybacks with my new net, and then I want to go out to the Fox and Hounds, and 'Don't-wake-Daddy!' she hissed angrily, clapping her hand across my mouth.

But it was too late. He was awake, or nearly so. He grunted and reached for the matches. Then he stared incredulously at his watch.

'Like a cup of tea, dear?' asked Mother in a meek, hushed voice I had never heard her use before. It sounded almost as though she were afraid.

'Tea?' he exclaimed indignantly. 'Do you know what the time is?'

'And after that I want to go up the Rathcooney Road,' I said loudly, afraid I'd forget something in all those interruptions.

'Go to sleep at once, Larry!' she said sharply.

I began to snivel. I couldn't concentrate, the way that pair went on, and smothering my early-morning schemes was like burying a family from the cradle.

Father said nothing, but lit his pipe and sucked it, looking out into the shadows without minding Mother or me. I knew he was mad. Every time I made a remark Mother hushed me irritably. I was mortified. I felt it wasn't fair; there was even something sinister in it. Every time I had pointed out to her the waste of making two beds when we could both sleep in one, she had told me it was healthier like that, and now here was this man, this stranger, sleeping with her without the least regard for her health! He got up early and made tea, but though he brought Mother a cup he brought none for me.

'Mummy,' I shouted, 'I want a cup of tea, too.'

'Yes, dear,' she said patiently. 'You can drink from Mummy's saucer.'

That settled it. Either Father or I would have to leave the house. I didn't want to drink from Mother's saucer; I wanted to be treated as an equal in my own home, so, just to spite her, I drank it all and left none for her. She took that quietly, too.

But that night when she was putting me to bed she said gently: 'Larry, I want you to promise me something.'

'What is it?' I asked.

'Not to come in and disturb poor Daddy in the morning. Promise?'

'Poor Daddy' again I was becoming suspicious of every thing involving that quite impossible man.

'Why?' I asked.

'Because poor Daddy is worried and tired and he doesn't sleep well'

'Why doesn't he, Mummy?'

'Well, you know, don't you, that while he was at the war Mummy got the pennies from the Post Office?'

'From Miss MacCarthy?'

'That's right. But now, you see, Miss MacCarthy hasn't any more pennies, so Daddy must go out and find us some. You know what would happen if he couldn't?'

'No,' I said, 'tell us.'

'Well, I think we might have to go out and beg for them like the poor old woman on Fridays We wouldn't like that, would we?'

'No,' I agreed. 'We wouldn't.'

'So you'll promise not to come in and wake him?'

'Promise.'

Mind you, I meant that. I knew pennies were a serious matter, and I was all against having to go out and beg like the old woman on Fridays. Mother laid out all my toys in a complete ring round the bed so that, whatever way I got out, I was bound to fall over one of them.

When I woke I remembered my promise all right. I got up and sat on the floor and played for hours, it seemed to me. Then I got my chair and looked out the attic window for more hours. I wished it was time for Father to wake; I wished someone would make me a cup of tea. I didn't feel in the least like the sun; instead, I was bored and so very, very cold! I simply longed for the warmth and depth of the big featherbed.

At last I could stand it no longer. I went into the next room. As there was still no room at Mother's side I climbed over her and she woke with a start.

'Larry,' she whispered, gripping my arm very tightly, 'what did you promise?'

'But I did, Mummy,' I wailed, caught in the very act. 'I was quiet for ever so long.'

'Oh, dear, and you're perished' she said sadly, feeling me all over. 'Now, if I let you stay will you promise not to talk?'

'But I want to talk, Mummy,' I wailed.

That has nothing to do with it,' she said with a firmness that was new to me. 'Daddy wants to sleep. Now, do you understand that?'

I understood it only too well. I wanted to talk, he wanted to sleep whose house was it, anyway?

'Mummy,' I said with equal firmness, 'I think it would be healthier for Daddy to sleep in his own bed.' That seemed to stagger her, because she said nothing for a while.

'Now, once for all,' she went on, 'you're to be perfectly quiet or go back to your own bed. Which is it to be?'

The injustice of it got me down. I had convicted her out of her own mouth of inconsistency and unreasonableness, and she hadn't even attempted to reply. Full of spite, I gave Father a kick, which she didn't notice but which made him grunt and open his eyes in alarm.

'What time is it?' he asked in a panic-stricken voice, not looking at Mother but at the door, as if he saw someone there.

'It's early yet,' she replied soothingly. 'It's only the child. Go to sleep again... Now, Larry,' she added, getting out of bed, 'you've wakened Daddy and you must go back.'

This time, for all her quiet air, I knew she meant it, and knew that my principal rights and privileges were as good as lost unless I asserted them at once. As she lifted me, I gave a screech, enough to wake the dead, not to mind Father. He groaned.

'That damn child! Doesn't he ever sleep?'

'It's only a habit, dear,' she said quietly, though I could see she was vexed.

'Well, it's time he got out of it,' shouted Father, beginning to heave in the bed. He suddenly gathered all the bedclothes about him, turned to the wall, and then looked back over his shoulder with nothing showing only two small, spiteful, dark eyes. The man looked very wicked.

To open the bedroom door, Mother had to let me down, and I broke free and dashed for the farthest corner, screeching. Father sat bolt upright in bed.

'Shut up, you little puppy!' he said in a choking voice.

I was so astonished that I stopped screeching. Never, never had anyone spoken to me in that tone before. I looked at him incredulously and saw his face convulsed with rage. It was only then that I fully realised how God had codded me, listening to my prayers for the safe return of this monster.

'Shut up, you!' I bawled, beside myself.

'What's that you said?' shouted Father, making a wild leap out of the bed.

'Mick, Mick!' cried Mother 'Don't you see the child isn't used to you?'

'I see he's better fed than taught,' snarled Father, waving his arms wildly. 'He wants his bottom smacked.'

All his previous shouting was as nothing to these obscene words referring to my person. They really made my blood boil.

'Smack your own!' I screamed hysterically. 'Smack your own! Shut up! Shut up!'

At this he lost his patience and let fly at me. He did it with the lack of conviction you'd expect of a man under Mother's horrified eyes, and it ended up as a mere tap, but the sheer indignity of being struck at all by a stranger, a total stranger who had cajoled his way back from the war into our big bed as a result of my innocent intercession, made me completely dotty. I shrieked and shrieked, and danced in my bare feet, and Father, looking awkward and hairy in nothing but a short grey army shirt, glared down at me like a mountain out for murder. I think it must have been then that I realised he was jealous too. And there stood Mother in her nightdress, looking as if her heart was broken between us. I hoped she felt as she looked. It seemed to me that she deserved it all.

From that morning out my life was a hell. Father and I were enemies, open and avowed. We conducted a series of skirmishes against one another, he trying to steal my time with Mother and I his. When she was sitting on my bed, telling me a story, he took to looking for some pair of old boots which he alleged he had left behind him at the beginning of the war. While he talked to

Mother I played loudly with my toys to show my total lack of concern. He created a terrible scene one evening when he came in from work and found me at his box, playing with his regimental badges, Gurkha knives, and button-sticks. Mother got up and took the box from me.

'You mustn't play with Daddy's toys unless he lets you, Larry,' she said severely. 'Daddy doesn't play with yours.'

For some reason Father looked at her as if she had struck him and then turned away with a scowl.

'Those are not toys,' he growled, taking down the box again to see had I lifted anything. 'Some of those curios are very rare and valuable.'

But as time went on I saw more and more how he managed to alienate Mother and me. What made it worse was that I couldn't grasp his method or see what attraction he had for Mother. In every possible way he was less winning than I. He had a common accent and made noises at his tea I thought for a while that it might be the newspapers she was interested in, so I made up bits of news of my own to read to her. Then I thought it might be the smoking, which I personally thought attractive, and took his pipes and went round the house dribbling into them till he caught me. I even made noises at my tea, but Mother only told me I was disgusting. It all seemed to hinge round that unhealthy habit of sleeping together, so I made a point of dropping into their bedroom and nosing round, talking to myself, so that they wouldn't know I was watching them, but they were never up to anything that I could see. In the end it beat me. It seemed to depend on being grown-up and giving people rings, and I realised I'd have to wait.

But at the same time I wanted him to see that I was only waiting, not giving up the fight. One evening when he was being particularly obnoxious, chattering away well above my head, I let him have it.

'Mummy,' I said, 'do you know what I'm going to do when I grow up?'

'No, dear,' she replied. 'What?'

'I'm going to marry you,' I said quietly.

Father gave a great guffaw out of him, but he didn't take me in. I knew it must only be pretence. And Mother, in spite of everything, was pleased. I felt she was probably relieved to know that one day Father's hold on her would be broken.

'Won't that be nice?' she said with a smile.

'It'll be very nice,' I said confidently. 'Because we're going to have lots and lots of babies.'

'That's right, dear,' she said placidly. 'I think we'll have one soon, and then you'll have plenty of company.'

I was no end pleased about that because it showed that in spite of the way she gave in to Father she still considered my wishes. Besides, it would put the Geneys in their place.

It didn't turn out like that, though. To begin with, she was very preoccupied I supposed about where she would get the seventeen and six and though Father took to staying out late in the evenings it did me no particular good. She stopped taking me for walks, became as touchy as blazes, and smacked me for nothing at all. Sometimes I wished I'd never mentioned the confounded baby I seemed to have a genius for bringing calamity on myself.

And calamity it was! Sonny arrived in the most appalling hullabaloo even that much he couldn't do without a fuss — and from the first moment I disliked him. He was a difficult child so far as I was concerned he was always difficult and demanded far too much attention. Mother was simply silly about him, and couldn't see when he was only showing off. As company he was worse than useless. He slept all day, and I had to go round the house on tiptoe to avoid waking him. It wasn't any longer a question of not waking Father. The slogan now was 'Don't-wake-Sonny!' I couldn't understand why the child wouldn't sleep at the proper time, so whenever Mother's back was turned I woke him. Sometimes to keep him awake I pinched him as well. Mother caught me at it one day and gave me a most unmerciful flaking.

One evening, when Father was coming in from work, I was playing trains in the front garden. I let on not to notice him;

instead, I pretended to be talking to myself, and said in a loud voice: 'If another bloody baby comes into this house, I'm going out.'

Father stopped dead and looked at me over his shoulder.

'What's that you said?' he asked sternly.

'I was only talking to myself,' I replied, trying to conceal my panic. 'It's private.'

He turned and went in without a word. Mind you, I intended it as a solemn warning, but its effect was quite different. Father started being quite nice to me. I could understand that, of course. Mother was quite sickening about Sonny. Even at mealtimes she'd get up and gawk at him in the cradle with an idiotic smile, and tell Father to do the same. He was always polite about it, but he looked so puzzled you could see he didn't know what she was talking about. He complained of the way Sonny cried at night, but she only got cross and said that Sonny never cried except when there was something up with him which was a flaming lie, because Sonny never had anything up with him, and only cried for attention. It was really painful to see how simple-minded she was. Father wasn't attractive, but he had a fine intelligence. He saw through Sonny, and now he knew that I saw through him as well.

One night I woke with a start. There was someone beside me in the bed. For one wild moment I felt sure it must be Mother, having come to her senses and left Father for good, but then I heard Sonny in convulsions in the next room, and Mother saying: 'There! There! There!' and I knew it wasn't she. It was Father. He was lying beside me, wide awake, breathing hard and apparently as mad as hell.

After a while it came to me what he was mad about. It was his turn now. After turning me out of the big bed, he had been turned out himself. Mother had no consideration now for anyone but that poisonous pup, Sonny. I couldn't help feeling sorry for Father. I had been through it all myself, and even at that age I was magnanimous. I began to stroke him down and say: 'There! There!' He wasn't exactly responsive.

'Aren't you asleep either?' he snarled.

'Ah, come on and put your arm around us, can't you?' I said, and he did, in a sort of way. Gingerly, I suppose, is how you'd describe it. He was very bony but better than nothing.

At Christmas he went out of his way to buy me a really nice model railway.

Old Fellows

If there was one thing I could not stand as a kid it was being taken out for the day by Father. My mature view is that he couldn't stand it either but did it to keep Mother quiet. Mother did it to keep him out of harm's way; I was supposed to act as a brake on him.

He always took me to the same place Crosshaven on the paddle-boat. He raved about Cork Harbour, its wonderful scenery and sea air. I was never one for scenery myself, and as for air, a little went a long way with me. With a man as unobservant as Father, buttons like mine, and strange boats and public-houses which I couldn't find my way about, I lived in mortal fear of an accident. One day in particular is always in my memory; a Sunday morning with the bells ringing for Mass and the usual scramble on to get Father out of the house. He was standing before the mirror which hung over the mantelpiece, dragging madly at his dickey, and Mother on a low stool in front of him, trying to fasten the studs.

'Ah, go easy!' she said impatiently. 'Go easy, can't you?'

Father couldn't go easy. He lowered his head all right, but he shivered and reared like a bucking bronco.

'God Almighty give me patience!' he hissed between his teeth. 'Give me patience, sweet God, before I tear the bloody house down!' It was never what you'd call a good beginning to the day. And to see him later, going down to Pope's Quay to Mass, you'd swear butter wouldn't melt in the old devil's mouth.

After Mass, as we were standing on the quay, J.J. came along. J.J. and Father were lifelong friends. He was a melancholy, reedy man with a long sallow face and big hollows under his cheeks. Whenever he was thinking deeply he sucked in the cheeks till his face caved in suddenly like a sandpit. We sauntered down a side street from the quay. I knew well where we were bound for, but with the incurable optimism of childhood I hoped again that this time we might be going somewhere else. We weren't. J.J. stopped by a door at a street corner and knocked softly. He had one ear cocked to the door and the other eye cocked at Father. A voice spoke within, a soft voice as in a confessional, and J.J. bowed his head reverently to the keyhole and whispered something back. Father raised his head with a smile and held up two fingers.

'Two minutes now!' he said, and then took a penny from his trouser pocket.

'There's a penny for you,' he said benignly. 'Mind now and be a good boy.'

The door opened and shut almost silently behind Father and J.J. I stood and looked round. The streets were almost deserted, and so silent you could hear the footsteps of people you couldn't see in the laneways high up the hill. The only living thing near me was a girl standing a little up from the street corner. She was wearing a frilly white hat and a white satiny dress. As it happened, I was wearing a sailor suit for the first time that day. It gave me a slightly raffish feeling. I went up to where she was standing, partly to see what she was looking at, partly to study her closer. She was a beautiful child upon my word, a beautiful child! And, whatever way it happened, I smiled at her. Mind you, I didn't mean any harm. It was pure good nature. To this day, that is the sort I am, wanting to be friends with everybody.

The little girl looked at me. She looked at me for a long time; long enough at any rate for the smile to wither off me, and then drew herself up with her head in the air and walked past me down the pavement. Looking back on it, I suppose she was upset because her own father was inside the pub, and a thing like that would mean more to a girl than a boy. But it wasn't only that. By nature she was haughty and cold. It was the first time I had come face to face with the heartlessness of real beauty, and her contemptuous stare knocked me flat. I was a sensitive child. I didn't know where to look, and I wished myself back at home with my mother.

After about ten minutes Father came out with his face all shiny and I ran up to him and took his hand. Unobservant and all as he was, he must have noticed I was upset, because he was suddenly full of palaver about the grand day we were going to have by the seaside. Of course it was all propaganda, because before we reached the boat at all, he had another call.

'Two minutes now!' he said with his two fingers raised and a roguish grin on his face. 'Definitely not more than two minutes! Be a good boy!'

At last we did get aboard the paddle-steamer, and, as we moved off down the river, people stood and waved from the road at Tivoli and from under the trees on the Marina walk, while the band played on deck. It was quite exciting, really. And then, all of a sudden, I saw coming up the deck towards us the little girl who had snubbed me outside the public-house. Her father was along with her, a small, fat, red-faced man with a big black beard and a bowler hat. He walked with a sort of roll, and under his arm he carried a model ship with masts and sails a really superior-looking ship which took my eye at once.

When my father saw him he gave a loud triumphant crow.

'We'll meet in heaven,' he said.

'I'd be surprised,' said the fat man none too pleasantly.

'Back to the old ship, I see?' said Father, giving J.J. a wink to show he could now expect some sport.

'What exactly do you mean by that?' asked the fat man, giving his moustache a twirl.

'My goodness,' said Father, letting on to be surprised, 'didn't you tell me 'twas aboard the paddle-boat in Cork Harbour you did your sailoring? Didn't you tell me yourself about the terrible storm that nearly wrecked ye between Aghada and Queenstown?'

'If I mentioned such a thing,' said the fat man, 'it was only in dread you mightn't have heard of any other place. You were never in Odessa, I suppose?'

'I had a cousin there,' said Father gravely. 'Cold, I believe. He was telling me they had to chop off the drinks with a hatchet'

'You hadn't a cousin in Valparaiso, by any chance?'

'Well, no, now,' said Father regretfully, 'that cousin died young of a Maltese fever he contracted while he was with Nansen at the North Pole.'

'Maltese fever!' snorted the fat man. 'I suppose you couldn't even tell me where Malta is.'

By this time there was no holding the pair of them. The fat man was a sailor, and whatever the reason was, my father couldn't see a sailor without wanting to be at his throat. They went into the saloon, and all the way down the river they never as much as stuck their noses out. When I looked in, half the bar had already joined in the argument, some in favour of going to sea and some, like Father, dead against it.

'It broadens the mind, I tell you,' said the sailor. 'Sailors see the world.'

'Do they, indeed?' said Father sarcastically.

'Malta,' said the sailor. 'You were talking about Malta. Now, there's a beautiful place. The heat of the day drives off the cold of the night.'

'Do it?' asked Father in a far-away voice, gazing out the door as though he expected someone to walk in. 'Anything else?'

'San Francisco,' said the sailor dreamily, 'and the scent of the orange blossoms in the moonlight.'

'Anything else?' Father asked remorselessly. He was like a priest in the confessional.

'As much more as you fancy,' said the sailor.

'But do they see what's under their very noses?' asked Father, rising with his eyes aglow. 'Do they see their own country? Do they see that river outside that people come thousands of miles to see? What old nonsense you have!'

I looked round and saw the little girl at my elbow.

'They're at it still,' I said.

''Tis all your fault,' she said coldly.

'How is it my fault?'

'You and your old fellow,' she said contemptuously. 'Ye have my day ruined on me.'   And away she walked again with her head in the air.

I didn't see her again until we landed, and by that time her father and mine had to be separated. They were on to politics, and J.J. thought it safer to get Father away. Father was all for William O'Brien, and he got very savage when he was contradicted. I watched the sailor and the little girl go off along the sea-road while we went in the opposite direction. Father was still simmering about things the sailor had said in favour of John Redmond, a politician he couldn't like. He suddenly stopped and raised his fists in the air.

'I declare to my God if there's one class of men I can't stand, 'tis sailors,' he said.

'They're all old blow,' agreed J.J. peaceably.

'I wouldn't mind the blooming blow,' Father said venomously. ''Tis all the lies they tell you. San Francisco? That fellow was never near San Francisco. Now, I'm going back,' he went on, beginning to stamp from one foot to the other, 'and *I'm* going to tell *him* a few lies for a change.'

'I wouldn't be bothered,' said J.J., and, leaning his head over Father's shoulder, he began to whisper in his ear the way you'd whisper to a restive young horse, and with the same sort of result, for Father gradually ceased his stamping and rearing and looked doubtfully at J.J. out of the corner of his eye. A moment later up went the two fingers.

'Two minutes,' he said with a smile that was only put on. 'Not more. Be a good boy now.'

He slipped me another copper and I sat on the sea-wall, watching the crowds and wondering if we'd ever get out of the village that day. Beyond the village were the cliffs, and pathways wound over them, in and out of groups of thatched cottages. The band would be playing up there, and people would be dancing. There would be stalls for lemonade and sweets. If only I could get up there I should at least have something to look at. My heart gave a jump and then sank. I saw, coming through the crowd, the sailor and the little girl. She was swinging out of his arm, and in her own free arm she carried the model ship. They stopped before the pub.

'Daddy,' I heard her say in that precise, ladylike little voice of hers, 'you promised to sail my boat for me.'

'In one second now,' said her father. 'I have a certain thing to say to a man in here.'

Then in with him to the pub. The little girl had tears in her eyes. I was sorry for her that's the sort I am, very soft-hearted.

'All right,' I said. 'I'll go in and try to get my da out.'

But when I went in I saw it was no good. Her father was sitting on the windowsill, and behind him the blue bay and the white yachts showed like a newspaper photo through the mesh of the window screen. Father was walking up and down, his head bent, like a caged tiger.

'Capwell?' I heard him say in a low voice.

'Capwell I said,' replied the sailor.

'Evergreen?' said Father.

'Evergreen,' nodded the sailor.

'The oldest stock in Cork, you said?' whispered Father.

'Fifteenth century,' said the sailor.

Father looked at him with a gathering smile as though he thought it was all one of the sailor's jokes. Then he shook his head good-humouredly, and walked to the other side of the bar as though to say it was too much for him. Madness had outranged itself.

'The north side of the city,' said the sailor, growing heated at such disbelief, 'what is it only foreigners? People that came in from beyond the lamps a generation ago. Tramps and fiddlers and pipers.'

'They had the intellect,' Father said quietly.

'Intellect?' exclaimed the sailor. 'The north side?'

'Twas always given up to them,' said Father firmly.

'That's the first I heard of it,' said the sailor.

Father began to scribble with a couple of fingers on the palm of his left hand.

'Now,' he said gravely, 'I'll give you fair odds. I'll go back a hundred years with you. Tell me the name of a single outstanding man now I said an *outstanding* man, mind you that was born on the south side of the city in that time.' 'Daddy,' I said, pulling him by the coat-tails, 'you promised to take me up the cliffs.' 'In two minutes now,' he replied with a brief laugh, and, almost by second nature, handed me another penny.

That was four I had. J.J., a thoughtful poor soul, followed me out with two bottles of lemonade and a couple of packets of biscuits. The little girl and I ate and drank, sitting on the low wall outside the pub. Then we went down to the water's edge and tried to sail the boat, but, whatever was wrong with it, it would only float on its side; its sails got wringing wet, and we left them to dry while we listened to the organ of the merry-go-rounds from the other side of the bay.

It wasn't until late afternoon that the sailor and Father came out, and by this time there seemed to be no more than the breath of life between them. It was astonishing to me how friendly they were. Father had the sailor by the lapel of the jacket and was begging him to wait for the boat, but the sailor explained that he had given his solemn word to his wife to have the little girl home in time for bed and insisted that he'd have to go by the train. After he had departed, my father threw a long, lingering look at the sky, and seeing it was so late, slipped me another penny and retired to the bar till the siren went for the boat. They were hauling up the gangway when J.J. got him down.

It was late when we landed, and the full moon was riding over the river; a lovely, nippy September night; but I was tired and hungry and blown up with wind. We went up the hill in the moonlight and every few yards Father stopped to lay down the law. By this time he was ready to argue with anyone about anything. We came to the cathedral, and there were three old women sitting on the steps gossiping, their black shawls trailing like shadows on the pavement. It made me sick for home, a cup of hot cocoa and my own warm bed.

Then suddenly under a gas lamp at the street-corner I saw a small figure in white. It was like an apparition. I was struck with terror and despair. I don't know if J.J. saw the same thing, but all at once he began to direct Father's attention to the cathedral and away from the figure in white.

'That's a beautiful tower,' he said in a husky voice.

Father stopped and screwed up his eyes to study it

'What's beautiful about it?' he asked. 'I don't see anything very remarkable about that.'

'Ah, 'tis, man,' said J.J. reverently. 'That's a great tower.'

'Now, I'm not much in favour of towers,' said Father, tossing his head cantankerously. 'I don't see what use are towers. I'd sooner a nice plain limestone front with pillars like the Sand Quay.'

At the time I wasn't very concerned about the merits of Gothic and Renaissance, so I tried to help J.J. by tugging Father's hand. It was no good. One glance round and his eye took in the white figure at the other side of the road. He chuckled ominously and put his hand over his eyes, like a sailor on deck.

'Hard a-port, mate!' he said. 'What do I see on my starboard bow?'

'Ah, nothing,' said J.J.

'Nothing?' echoed Father joyously. 'What sort of lookout man are you? ... Ahoy, shipmate!' he bawled across the road. 'Didn't your old skipper go home yet?'

'He did not,' cried the little girl it was she of course 'and let you leave him alone!'

'The thundering ruffian!' said my father in delight, and away he went across the road. 'What do he mean? A sailorman from the south side, drinking in my diocese! I'll have him ejected.'

'Daddy,' I wailed, with my heart in my boots. 'Come home, can't you?'

'Two minutes,' he said with a chuckle, and handed me another copper, the sixth.

The little girl was frantic. She scrawled and beat him about the legs with her fist, but he only laughed at her, and when the door opened he forced his way in with a shout: 'Anyone here from Valparaiso?'

J.J. sucked in his cheeks till he looked like a skeleton in the moonlight, and then nodded sadly and followed Father in. The door was bolted behind them and the little girl and I were left together on the pavement. The three old women on the cathedral steps got up and shuffled off down a cobbled laneway. The pair of us sat on the kerb and snivelled.

'What bad luck was on me this morning to meet you?' said the little girl.

''Twas on me the bad luck was,' I said, 'and your old fellow keeping my old fellow out.'

'Your old fellow is only a common labouring man,' said the little girl contemptuously, 'and my daddy says he's ignorant and conceited.'

'And your old fellow is only a sailor,' I retorted indignantly, 'and my father says all sailors are liars.'

'How dare you!' she said. 'My daddy is not a liar, and I hope he keeps your fellow inside all night, just to piece you out for your impudence.'

'I don't care,' I said with mock bravado. 'I can go home when I like and you can't bah!'

'You'll have to wait till your father comes out.'

'I needn't. I can go home myself.'

'I dare you! You and your sailor suit!'

I could have let it pass but for her gibe at my suit; but that insult had to be avenged. I got up and took a few steps, just to show her. I thought she'd be afraid to stay behind alone, but she wasn't She was too bitter. Of course, I had no intention of going home by myself at that hour of night. I stopped.

'Coward!' she said venomously. 'You're afraid.'

'I'll show you whether I'm afraid or not,' I said sulkily, and went off down Shandon Street I who had never before been out alone after dark. I was terrified. It's no use swanking about it. I was simply terrified. I stopped every few yards, hoping she'd call out or that Father would come running after me. Neither happened, and at each dark laneway I shut my eyes. There was no sound but feet climbing this flight of steps or descending that. When I reached the foot of Shandon Street by the old graveyard, and saw the long, dark, winding hill before me, my courage gave out. I was afraid to go on and afraid to turn back.

Then I saw a friendly sign; a little huxter shop with a long flight of steps to the door, flanked by iron railings. High over the basement I could see the narrow window decorated in crinkly red paper, with sweet bottles and a few toys on view. Then I saw one toy that raised my courage. I counted my coppers again. There were six. I climbed the steps, went in the dark hallway, and turned right into the front room, which was used as the shop. A little old Mother Hubbard of a woman came out, rubbing her hands in her apron.

'Well, little boy?' she asked briskly.

'I want a dog, ma'am.'

'Sixpence apiece the dogs,' she said doubtfully. 'Have you sixpence?'

'I have, ma'am,' said I, and I counted out my coppers. She gave me the dog, a black, woolly dog with two beads for ears. I ran down the steps and up the road with my head high, whistling. I only wished that the little girl could see me now; she wouldn't say I was a coward. To show my contempt for the terrors of night I stood at the mouth of each laneway and looked down. I stroked the dog's fur, and when some shadow loomed up more frightening than the others I turned his head at it.

'Ssss!' I said. 'At him, boy! At him!'

When Mother opened the door I caught him and held him back.

'Down, Towser, down!' I said commandingly. 'It's only Mummy.'

The Study of History

The discovery of where babies came from filled my life with
excitement and interest. Not in the way it's generally supposed
to of course. Oh, no! I never seem to have done anything like a
natural child in a standard textbook I merely discovered the
fascination of history. Up to this I had lived in a country of my
own that had no history, and accepted my parents' marriage as
an event ordained from the creation; now, when I considered it
in this new, scientific way, I began to see it merely as one of the
turning-points of history; one of those apparently trivial events
that are little more than accidents, but have the effect of changing
the destiny of humanity. I had not heard of Pascal, but I would
have approved his remark about what would have happened if
Cleopatra's nose had been a bit longer.

It immediately changed my view of my parents. Up to this they
had been principles, not characters, like a chain of mountains
guarding a green horizon. Suddenly a little shaft of light, emerging from behind a cloud, struck them, and the whole mass broke
up into peaks, valleys, and foothills; you could even see white-
washed farmhouses and fields where people worked in the
evening light, a whole world of interior perspective. Mother's
past was the richer subject for study. It was extraordinary the
variety of people and settings that woman had in her back-
ground. She had been an orphan, a parlour maid, a companion,
a traveller; and had been proposed to by a plasterer's apprentice,
a French chef who had taught her to make superb coffee, and a
rich elderly shopkeeper in Sunday's Well. Because I liked to feel
myself different, I thought a great deal about the chef and the
advantages of being a Frenchman, but the shopkeeper was an
even more vivid figure in my imagination because he had married
someone else and died soon after of disappointment, I had no
doubt leaving a large fortune. The fortune was to me what

Cleopatra's nose was to Pascal; the ultimate proof that things might have been different.

'How much was Mr Riordan's fortune, Mummy?' I asked thoughtfully.

'Ah, they said he left eleven thousand,' Mother replied doubtfully, 'but you couldn't believe everything people say.'

That was exactly what I could do. I was not prepared to minimise a fortune that I might so easily have inherited.

'And weren't you ever sorry for poor Mr Riordan?' I asked severely.

'Ah, why would I be sorry, child?' she asked with a shrug. 'Sure, what use would money be where there was no liking?'

That, of course, was not what I meant at all. My heart was full of pity for poor Mr Riordan who had tried to be my father; but, even on the low level at which Mother discussed it, money would have been of great use to me. I was not so fond of Father as to think he was worth eleven thousand pounds, a hard sum to visualise but more than twenty-seven times greater than the largest salary I had ever heard of that of a Member of Parliament. One of the discoveries I was making at the time was that Mother was not only rather hardhearted but very impractical as well.

But Father was the real surprise. He was a brooding, worried man who seemed to have no proper appreciation of me, and was always wanting me to go out and play or go upstairs and read, but the historical approach changed him like a character in a fairy-tale.

'Now let's talk about the ladies Daddy nearly married,' I would say; and he would stop whatever he was doing and give a great guffaw. 'Oh, ho, ho!' he would say, slapping his knee and looking slyly at Mother, 'you could write a book about them.' Even his face changed at such moments. He would look young and extraordinarily mischievous. Mother, on the other hand, would grow black.

'You could,' she would say, looking into the fire. 'Daisies!'

'"The handsomest man that walks Cork!"' Father would quote with a wink at me. 'That's what one of them called me.'

'Yes,' Mother would say, scowling. 'May Cadogan!'

'The very girl!' Father would cry in astonishment. 'How did I forget her name? A beautiful girl! 'Pon my word, a most remarkable girl! And still is, I hear.'

'She should be,' Mother would say in disgust. 'With six of them!'

'Oh, now, she'd be the one that could look after them! A fine head that girl had.'

'She had. I suppose she ties them to a lamp-post while she goes in to drink and gossip.'

That was one of the peculiar things about history. Father and Mother both loved to talk about it but in different ways. She would only talk about it when we were together somewhere, in the park or down the Glen, and even then it was very hard to make her stick to the facts, because her whole face would light up and she would begin to talk about donkey-carriages or concerts in the kitchen, or oil-lamps, and though nowadays I would probably value it for atmosphere, in those days it sometimes drove me mad with impatience. Father, on the other hand, never minded talking about it in front of her, and it made her angry. Particularly when he mentioned May Cadogan. He knew this perfectly well and he would wink at me and make me laugh outright, though I had no idea of why I laughed, and anyway, my sympathy was all with her.

'But, Daddy,' I would say, presuming on his high spirits, 'if you liked Miss Cadogan so much why didn't you marry her?'

At this, to my great delight, he would let on to be filled with doubt and distress. He would put his hands in his trousers pockets and stride to the door leading into the hallway.

'That was a delicate matter,' he would say, without looking at me. 'You see, I had your poor mother to think of.'

'I was a great trouble to you,' Mother would say, in a blaze.

'Poor May said it to me herself,' he would go on as though he had not heard her, 'and the tears pouring down her cheeks. "Mick," she said, "that girl with the brown hair will bring me to an untimely grave." '

'She could talk of hair!' Mother would hiss. 'With her carroty mop!'

'Never did I suffer the way I suffered then, between the two of them,' Father would say with deep emotion as he returned to his chair by the window.

'Oh, 'tis a pity about ye!' Mother could cry in an exasperated tone and suddenly get up and go into the front room with her book to escape his teasing. Every word that man said she took literally. Father would give a great guffaw of delight, his hands on his knees and his eyes on the ceiling and wink at me again. I would laugh with him of course, and then grow wretched because I hated Mother's sitting alone in the front room. I would go in and find her in her wicker-chair by the window in the dusk, the book open on her knee, looking out at the Square. She would always have regained her composure when she spoke to me, but I would have an uncanny feeling of unrest in her and stroke her and talk to her soothingly as if we had changed places and I were the adult and she the child.

But if I was excited by what history meant to them, I was even more excited by what it meant to me. My potentialities were double theirs. Through Mother I might have been a French boy called Laurence Armady or a rich boy from Sunday's Well called Laurence Riordan. Through Father I might, while still remaining a Delaney, have been one of the six children of the mysterious and beautiful Miss Cadogan. I was fascinated by the problem of who I would have been if I hadn't been me, and, even more, by the problem of whether or not I would have known that there was anything wrong with the arrangement. Naturally I tended to regard Laurence Delaney as the person I was intended to be, and so I could not help wondering whether as Laurence Riordan I would not have been aware of Laurence Delaney as a real gap in my make-up.

I remember that one afternoon after school I walked by myself all the way up to Sunday's Well which I now regarded as something like a second home. I stood for a while at the garden gate of the house where Mother had been working when she was proposed to by Mr Riordan, and then went and studied the shop itself. It had clearly seen better days, and the cartons and advertisements in the window were dusty and sagging. It wasn't like one of the big stores in Patrick Street, but at the same time, in size and fittings it was well above the level of a village shop. I regretted that Mr Riordan was dead because I would like to have seen him for myself instead of relying on Mother's impressions which seemed to me to be biased. Since he had, more or less, died of grief on Mother's account, I conceived of him as a really nice man; lent him the countenance and manner of an old gentleman who always spoke to me when he met me on the road, and felt I could have become really attached to him as a father. I could imagine it all: Mother reading in the parlour while she waited for me to come home up Sunday's Well in a school cap and blazer, like the boys from the Grammar School, and with an expensive leather satchel instead of the old cloth school-bag I carried over my shoulder. I could see myself walking slowly and with a certain distinction, lingering at gateways and looking down at the river; and later I would go out to tea in one of the big houses with long gardens sloping to the water, and maybe row a boat on the river along with a girl in a pink frock. I wondered only whether I would have any awareness of the National School boy with the cloth school-bag who jammed his head between the bars of a gate and thought of me. It was a queer, lonesome feeling that all but reduced me to tears.

But the place that had the greatest attraction of all for me was the Douglas Road where Father's friend, Miss Cadogan, lived, only now she wasn't Miss Cadogan but Mrs O'Brien. Naturally, nobody called Mr's O'Brien could be as attractive to the imagination as a French chef and an elderly shopkeeper with eleven thousand pounds, but she had a physical reality that the other pair lacked. As I went early to the library at Parnell Bridge, I frequently found myself wandering up the road in the direction of Douglas and always stopped in front of the long row of houses where she lived. There were high steps up to them, and in the evening the sunlight fell brightly on the house-fronts till they

looked like a screen. One evening as I watched a gang of boys
playing ball in the street outside, curiosity overcame me. I spoke
to one of them. Having been always a child of solemn and
unnatural politeness, I probably scared the wits out of him.

'I wonder if you could tell me which house Mrs O'Brien lives in,
please?' I asked.

'Hi, Gussie!' he yelled to another boy. 'This fellow wants to know
where your old one lives.'

This was more than I had bargained for. Then a thin, good-
looking boy of about my own age detached himself from the
group and came up to me with his fists clenched. I was feeling
distinctly panicky, but all the same I studied him closely. After
all, he was the boy I might have been.

'What do you want to know for?' he asked suspiciously.

Again, this was something I had not anticipated.

'My father was a great friend of your mother,' I explained
carefully, but, so far as he was concerned, I might as well have
been talking a foreign language. It was clear that Gussie O'Brien
had no sense of history.

'What's that?' he asked incredulously.

At this point we were interrupted by a woman I had noticed
earlier, talking to another over the railing between the two steep
gardens. She was a small, untidy-looking woman who occasionally rocked the pram in an absent-minded way as though she only
remembered it at intervals.

'What is it, Gussie?' she cried, raising herself on tiptoe to see us
better.

'I don't really want to disturb your mother, thank you,' I said, in
something like hysterics, but Gussie anticipated me, actually
pointing me out to her in a manner I had been brought up to
regard as rude.

'This fellow wants you,' he bawled.

'I don't really,' I murmured, feeling that now I was in for it. She
slipped down the high flight of steps to the gate with a laughing,
puzzled air, her eyes in slits and her right hand arranging her hair

at the back. It was not carroty as Mother described it, though it had red lights when the sun caught it.

'What is it, little boy?' she asked coaxingly, bending forward.

'I didn't really want anything, thank you,' I said in terror. 'It was just that my daddy said you lived up here, and, as I was changing my book at the library I thought I'd come up and inquire. You can see,' I added, showing her the book as proof, 'that I've only just been to the library.'

'But who is your daddy, little boy?' she asked, her grey eyes still in long, laughing slits. 'What's your name?'

'My name is Delaney,' I said, 'Larry Delaney.'

'Not Mike Delaney's boy?' she exclaimed wonderingly. 'Well, for God's sake! Sure, I should have known it from that big head of yours.' She passed her hand down the back of my head and laughed. 'If you'd only get your hair cut I wouldn't be long recognising you. You wouldn't think I'd know the feel of your old fellow's head, would you?' she added roguishly.

'No, Mrs O'Brien,' I replied meekly.

'Why, then indeed I do, and more along with it,' she added in the same saucy tone though the meaning of what she said was not clear to me. 'Ah, come in and give us a good look at you! That's my eldest, Gussie, you were talking to,' she added, taking my hand. Gussie trailed behind us for a purpose I only recognised later.

'Ma-a-a-a, who's dat fella with you?' yelled a fat little girl who had been playing hop-scotch on the pavement.

'That's Larry Delaney,' her mother sang over her shoulder. I don't know what it was about that woman but there was something about her high spirits that made her more like a regiment than a woman. You felt that everyone should fall into step behind her. 'Mick Delaney's son from Barrackton. I nearly married his old fellow once. Did he ever tell you that, Larry?' she added slyly. She made sudden swift transitions from brilliance to intimacy that I found attractive.

'Yes, Mrs O'Brien, he did,' I replied, trying to sound as roguish as she, and she went off into a delighted laugh, tossing her red head.

'Ah, look at that now! How well the old divil didn't forget me! You can tell him I didn't forget him either. And if I married him, I'd be your mother now. Wouldn't that be a queer old three and fourpence? How would you like me for a mother, Larry?'

'Very much, thank you,' I said complacently.

'Ah, go on with you, you would not,' she exclaimed, but she was pleased all the same. She struck me as the sort of woman it would be easy enough to please. 'Your old fellow always said it: your mother was a *most* superior woman, and you're a *most* superior child. Ah, and I'm not too bad myself either,' she added with a laugh and a shrug, wrinkling up her merry little face.

In the kitchen she cut me a slice of bread, smothered it with jam, and gave me a big mug of milk. 'Will you have some, Gussie?' she asked in a sharp voice as if she knew only too well what the answer would be. 'Aideen,' she said to the horrible little girl who had followed us in, 'aren't you fat and ugly enough without making a pig of yourself? Murder the Loaf we call her,' she added smilingly to me. 'You're a polite little boy, Larry, but damn the politeness you'd have if you had to deal with them. Is the book for your mother?'

'Oh, no, Mrs O'Brien,' I replied. 'It's my own.'

'You mean you can read a big book like that?' she asked incredulously, taking it from my hands and measuring the length of it with a puzzled air.

'Oh, yes, I can.'

'I don't believe you,' she said mockingly. 'Go on and prove it!' There was nothing I asked better than to prove it. I felt that as a performer I had never got my due, so I stood in the middle of the kitchen, cleared my throat and began with great feeling to enunciate one of those horribly involved opening paragraphs you found in children's books of the time. 'On a fine evening in spring, as the setting sun was beginning to gild the blue peaks with its lambent rays, a rider, recognisable as a student by certain niceties of attire, was slowly, and perhaps regretfully making his way ...' It was the sort of opening sentence I loved.

'I declare to God!' Mrs O'Brien interrupted in astonishment. 'And that fellow there is one age with you, and he can't spell house. How well you wouldn't be down at the library, you caubogue you!... That's enough now, Larry,' she added hastily as I made ready to entertain them further.

'Who wants to read that blooming old stuff?' Gussie said contemptuously. Later, he took me upstairs to show me his air rifle and model aeroplanes. Every detail of the room is still clear to me: the view into the back garden with its jungle of wild plants where Gussie had pitched his tent (a bad site for a tent as I patiently explained to him, owing to the danger from wild beasts); the three cots still unmade, the scribbles on the walls, and Mrs O'Brien's voice from the kitchen calling to Aideen to see what was wrong with the baby who was screaming his head off from the pram outside the front door. Gussie, in particular, fascinated me. He was spoiled, clever, casual; good-looking, with his mother's small clean features; gay and calculating. I saw that when I left and his mother gave me sixpence. Naturally I refused it politely, but she thrust it into my trousers pocket, and Gussie dragged at her skirt, noisily demanding something for himself. 'If you give him a tanner you ought to give me a tanner,' he yelled. 'I'll tan you,' she said laughingly.

'Well, give us a lop anyway,' he begged, and she did give him a penny to take his face off her, as she said herself, and after that he followed me down the street and suggested we should go to the shop and buy sweets. I was simple-minded, but I wasn't an out-and-out fool, and I knew that if I went to a sweet-shop with Gussie I should end up with no sixpence and very few sweets. So I told him I could not buy sweets without Mother's permission, at which he gave me up altogether as a cissy or worse.

It had been an exhausting afternoon but a very instructive one. In the twilight I went back slowly over the bridges, a little regretful for that fast-moving, colourful household, but with a new appreciation of my own home. When I went in the lamp was lit over the fireplace and Father was at his tea.

'What kept you, child?' Mother asked with an anxious air, and suddenly I felt slightly guilty, and I played it as I usually did whenever I was at fault in a loud, demonstrative, grownup way. I stood in the middle of the kitchen with my cap in my hand and pointed it first at one, then at the other.

'You wouldn't believe who I met!' I said dramatically.

'Wisha, who, child?' Mother asked.

'Miss Cadogan,' I said, placing my cap squarely on a chair and turning on them both again. 'Miss May Cadogan. Mrs O'Brien as she is now.'

'Mrs O'Brien?' Father exclaimed, putting down his cup. 'But where did you meet Mrs O'Brien?'

'I said you wouldn't believe it. It was near the library. I was talking to some fellows, and what do you think but one of them was Gussie O'Brien, Mrs O'Brien's son. And he took me home with him, and his mother gave me bread and jam, and she gave me THIS.' I produced the sixpence with a real flourish.

'Well, I'm blowed!' Father gasped, and first he looked at me, and then he looked at Mother and burst into a loud guffaw.

'And she said to tell you she remembers you too, and that she sent her love.'

'Oh, by the jumping bell of Athlone!' Father crowed and clapped his hands on his knees. I could see he believed the story I had told and was delighted with it, and I could see too that Mother did not believe it and that she was not in the least delighted. That, of course, was the trouble with Mother. Though she would do anything to help me with an intellectual problem, she never seemed to understand the need for experiment. She never opened her mouth while Father cross questioned me, shaking his head in wonder and storing it up to tell the men in the factory. What pleased him most was Mrs O'Brien's remembering the shape of his head, and later, while Mother was out of the kitchen, I caught him looking in the mirror and stroking the back of his head.

But I knew too that for the first time I had managed to produce in Mother the unrest that Father could produce, and I felt wretched and guilty and didn't know why. That was an aspect of history I only studied later.

That night I was really able to indulge my passion. At last I had the material to work with. I saw myself as Gussie O'Brien, standing in the bedroom, looking down at my tent in the garden, and Aideen as my sister, and Mrs O'Brien as my mother and, like Pascal, I re-created history. I remembered Mrs O'Brien's laughter, her scolding and the way she stroked my head. I knew she was kind casually kind and hot-tempered, and recognised that in dealing with her I must somehow be a different sort of person. Being good at reading would never satisfy her. She would almost compel you to be as Gussie was; flattering, impertinent, and exacting. Though I couldn't have expressed it in those terms, she was the sort of woman who would compel you to flirt with her. Then, when I had had enough, I deliberately soothed myself as I did whenever I had scared myself by pretending that there was a burglar in the house or a wild animal trying to get in the attic window. I just crossed my hands on my chest, looked up at the window and said to myself: 'It is not like that. I am not Gussie O'Brien. I am Larry Delaney, and my mother is Mary Delaney, and we live in Number 8 Wellington Square. Tomorrow I'll go to school at the Cross, and first there will be prayers, and then arithmetic and after that composition.'

For the first time the charm did not work. I had ceased to be Gussie all right, but somehow I had not become myself again, not any self that I knew. It was as though my own identity was a sort of sack I had to live in, and I had deliberately worked my way out of it, and now I couldn't get back again because I had grown too big for it. I practised every trick I knew to reassure myself. I tried to play a counting game; then I prayed, but even the prayer seemed different as though it didn't belong to me at all. I was away in the middle of empty space, divorced from my mother and home and everything permanent and familiar. Suddenly I found myself sobbing. The door opened and Mother came in in her nightdress, shivering, her hair over her face.

'You're not sleeping, child,' she said in a wan and complaining voice.

I snivelled, and she put her hand on my forehead.

'You're hot,' she said. 'What ails you?'

I could not tell her of the nightmare in which I was lost. Instead, I took her hand, and gradually the terror retreated, and I became myself again, shrank into my little skin of identity, and left infinity and all its anguish behind.

'Mummy,' I said, 'I promise I never wanted anyone but you.'

The Drunkard

It was a terrible blow to Father when Mr Dooley on the terrace died. Mr Dooley was a commercial traveller with two sons in the Dominicans and a car of his own, so socially he was miles ahead of us, but he had no false pride. Mr Dooley was an intellectual, and, like all intellectuals, the thing he loved best was conversation, and in his own limited way Father was a well-read man and could appreciate an intelligent talker. Mr Dooley was remarkably intelligent. Between business acquaintances and clerical contacts, there was very little he didn't know about what went on in town, and evening after evening he crossed the road to our gate to explain to Father the news behind the news. He had a low, palavering voice and a knowing smile, and Father would listen in astonishment, giving him a conversational lead now and again, and then stump triumphantly in to Mother with his face aglow and ask: 'Do you know what Mr Dooley is after telling me?' Ever since, when somebody has given me some bit of information off the record I have found myself on the point of asking: 'Was it Mr Dooley told you that?'

Till I actually saw him laid out in his brown shroud with the rosary beads entwined between his waxy fingers I did not take the report of his death seriously. Even then I felt there must be a catch and that some summer evening Mr Dooley must reappear at our gate to give us the lowdown on the next world. But Father was very upset, partly because Mr Dooley was about one age with himself, a thing that always gives a distinctly personal turn to another man's demise; partly because now he would have no one to tell him what dirty work was behind the latest scene at the Corporation. You could count on your fingers the number of men in Blarney Lane who read the papers as Mr Dooley did, and none of these would have overlooked the fact that Father was only a labouring man. Even Sullivan, the carpenter, a mere nobody, thought he was a cut above Father. It was certainly a solemn event.

'Half past two to the Curragh,' Father said meditatively, putting down the paper.

'But you're not thinking of going to the funeral?' Mother asked in alarm.

''Twould be expected,' Father said, scenting opposition. 'I wouldn't give it to say to them.'

'I think,' said Mother with suppressed emotion, 'it will be as much as anyone will expect if you go to the chapel with him.'

('Going to the chapel', of course, was one thing, because the body was removed after work, but going to a funeral meant the loss of a half-day's pay.)

'The people hardly know us,' she added.

'God between us and all harm,' Father replied with dignity, 'we'd be glad if it was our own turn.'

To give Father his due, he was always ready to lose a halfday for the sake of an old neighbour. It wasn't so much that he liked funerals as that he was a conscientious man who did as he would be done by; and nothing could have consoled him so much for the prospect of his own death as the assurance of a worthy funeral. And, to give Mother her due, it wasn't the halfday's pay she begrudged, badly as we could afford it.

Drink, you see, was Father's great weakness. He could keep steady for months, even for years, at a stretch, and while he did he was as good as gold. He was first up in the morning and brought the mother a cup of tea in bed, stayed at home in the evenings and read the paper; saved money and bought himself a new blue serge suit and bowler hat. He laughed at the folly of men who, week in week out, left their hard-earned money with the publicans; and sometimes, to pass an idle hour, he took pencil and paper and calculated precisely how much he saved each week through being a teetotaller. Being a natural optimist he sometimes continued this calculation through the whole span of his prospective existence and the total was breathtaking. He would die worth hundreds.

If I had only known it, this was a bad sign; a sign he was becoming stuffed up with spiritual pride and imagining himself better than his neighbours. Sooner or later, the spiritual pride grew till it called for some form of celebration. Then he took a drink not whiskey, of course; nothing like that just a glass of some harmless drink like lager beer. That was the end of Father. By the time he had taken the first he already realised that he had made a fool of himself, took a second to forget it and a third to forget that he couldn't forget, and at last came home reeling drunk. From this on it was 'The Drunkard's Progress', as in the moral prints. Next day he stayed in from work with a sick head while Mother went off to make his excuses at the works, and inside a fortnight he was poor and savage and despondent again. Once he began he drank steadily through everything down to the kitchen clock. Mother and I knew all the phases and dreaded all the dangers. Funerals were one.

'I have to go to Dunphy's to do a half-day's work,' said Mother in distress. 'Who's to look after Larry?'

'I'll look after Larry,' Father said graciously. 'The little walk will do him good.'

There was no more to be said, though we all knew I didn't need anyone to look after me, and that I could quite well have stayed at home and looked after Sonny, but I was being attached to the party to act as a brake on Father. As a brake I had never achieved anything, but Mother still had great faith in me.

Next day, when I got home from school, Father was there before me and made a cup of tea for both of us. He was very good at tea, but too heavy in the hand for anything else; the I way he cut bread was shocking. Afterwards we went down the hill to the church, Father wearing his best blue serge and a bowler cocked to one side of his head with the least suggestion of the masher. To his great joy he discovered Peter Crowley among the mourners. Peter was another danger signal, as I knew well from certain experiences after Mass on Sunday morning: a mean man, as Mother said, who only went to funerals for the free drinks he could get at them. It turned out that he hadn't even known Mr Dooley! But Father had a sort of contemptuous regard for him as one of the foolish people who wasted their good money in public-houses when they could be saving it. Very little of his own money Peter Crowley wasted!

It was an excellent funeral from Father's point of view. He had it all well studied before we set off after the hearse in the afternoon sunlight.

'Five carriages!' he exclaimed. 'Five carriages and sixteen covered cars! There's one alderman, two councillors and 'tis unknown how many priests. I didn't see a funeral like this from the road since Willie Mack, the publican died.'

'Ah, he was well liked,' said Crowley in his husky voice.

'My goodness, don't I know that?' snapped Father. 'Wasn't the man my best friend? Two nights before he died only two nights he was over telling me the goings-on about the housing contract. Them fellows in the Corporation are night and day robbers. But even I never imagined he was as well connected as that.'

Father was stepping out like a boy, pleased with everything: the other mourners, and the fine houses along Sunday's Well. I knew the danger signals were there in full force: a sunny day, a fine funeral, and a distinguished company of clerics and public men were bringing out all the natural vanity and flightiness of Father's character. It was with something like genuine pleasure that he saw his old friend lowered into the grave; with the sense of having performed a duty and the pleasant awareness that however much he would miss poor Mr Dooley in the long summer evenings, it was he and not poor Mr Dooley who would do the missing.

'We'll be making tracks before they break up,' he whispered to Crowley as the gravediggers tossed in the first shovelfuls of clay, and away he went, hopping like a goat from grassy hump to hump. The drivers, who were probably in the same state as himself, though without months of abstinence to put an edge on it, looked up hopefully.

'Are they nearly finished, Mick?' bawled one.

'All over now bar the last prayers,' trumpeted Father in the tone of one who brings news of great rejoicing.

The carriages passed us in a lather of dust several hundred yards from the public-house, and Father, whose feet gave him trouble in hot weather, quickened his pace, looking nervously over his shoulder for any sign of the main body of mourners crossing the hill. In a crowd like that a man might be kept waiting. When we did reach the pub the carriages were drawn up outside, and solemn men in black ties were cautiously bringing out consolation to mysterious females whose hands reached out modestly from behind the drawn blinds of the coaches. Inside the pub there were only the drivers and a couple of shawly women. I felt if I was to act as a brake at all, this was the time, so I pulled Father by the coat-tails.

'Dadda, can't we go home now?' I asked.

'Two minutes now,' he said, beaming affectionately. 'Just a bottle of lemonade and we'll go home.'

This was a bribe, and I knew it, but I was always a child of weak character. Father ordered lemonade and two pints. I was thirsty and swallowed my drink at once. But that wasn't Father's way. He had long months of abstinence behind him and an eternity of pleasure before. He took out his pipe, blew through it, filled it, and then lit it with loud pops, his eyes bulging above it. After that he deliberately turned his back on the pint, leaned one elbow on the counter in the attitude of a man who did not know there was a pint behind him, and deliberately brushed the tobacco from his palms. He had settled down for the evening. He was steadily working through all the important funerals he had ever attended. The carriages departed and the minor mourners drifted in till the pub was half full.

'Dadda,' I said, pulling his coat again, 'can't we go home now?'

'Ah, your mother won't be in for a long time yet,' he said benevolently enough. 'Run out in the road and play, can't you?' It struck me as very cool, the way grown-ups assumed that you could play all by yourself on a strange road. I began to get bored as I had so often been bored before. I knew Father was quite capable of lingering there till nightfall. I knew I might have to bring him home, blind drunk, down Blarney Lane, with all the old women at their doors, saying: 'Mick Delaney is on it again.' I knew that my mother would be half crazy with anxiety; that next day Father wouldn't go out to work; and before the end of the week she would be running down to the pawn with the clock under her shawl. I could never get over the lonesomeness of the kitchen without a clock.

I was still thirsty. I found if I stood on tiptoe I could just reach Father's glass, and the idea occurred to me that it would be interesting to know what the contents were like. He had his back to it and wouldn't notice. I took down the glass and sipped cautiously. It was a terrible disappointment. I was astonished that he could even drink such stuff. It looked as if he had never tried lemonade.

I should have advised him about lemonade but he was holding forth himself in great style. I heard him say that bands were a great addition to a funeral. He put his arms in the position of someone holding a rifle in reverse and hummed a few bars of Chopin's Funeral March. Crowley nodded reverently. I took a longer drink and began to see that porter might have its advantages. I felt pleasantly elevated and philosophic. Father hummed a few bars of the Dead March in Saul. It was a nice pub and a very fine funeral, and I felt sure that poor Mr Dooley in Heaven must be highly gratified. At the same time I thought they might have given him a band. As Father said, bands were a great addition. But the wonderful thing about porter was the way it made you stand aside, or rather float aloft like a cherub rolling on a cloud, and watch yourself with your legs crossed, leaning against a bar counter, not worrying about trifles but thinking deep, serious, grown-up thoughts about life and death. Looking at yourself like that, you couldn't help thinking after a while how funny you looked, and suddenly you got embarrassed and wanted to giggle. But by the time I had finished the pint, that phase too had passed; I found it hard to put back the glass, the counter seemed to have grown so high. Melancholia was supervening again.

'Well,' Father said reverently, reaching behind him for his drink, 'God rest the poor man's soul, wherever he is.' He stopped, looked first at the glass, and then at the people round him. 'Hello,' he said in a fairly good-humoured tone, as if he were just prepared to consider it a joke, even if it was in bad taste, 'who was at this?'

There was silence for a moment while the publican and the old women looked first at Father and then at his glass.

'There was no one at it, my good man,' one of the women said with an offended air. 'Is it robbers you think we are?'

'Ah, there's no one here would do a thing like that, Mick,' said the publican in a shocked tone.

'Well, someone did it,' said Father, his smile beginning to wear off.

'If they did, they were them that were nearer it,' said the woman darkly, giving me a dirty look; and at the same moment the truth began to dawn on Father. I suppose I must have looked a bit starry-eyed. He bent and shook me.

'Are you all right, Larry?' he asked in alarm.

Peter Crowley looked down at me and grinned.

'Could you beat that?' he exclaimed in a husky voice.

I could, and without difficulty. I started to get sick. Father jumped back in holy terror that I might spoil his good suit, and hastily opened the back door.

'Run! run! run!' he shouted.

I saw the sunlit wall outside with the ivy overhanging it, and ran. The intention was good but the performance was exaggerated, because I lurched right into the wall, hurting it badly, as it seemed to me. Being always very polite, I said 'Pardon' before the second bout came on me. Father, still concerned for his suit, came up behind and cautiously held me while I got sick.

'That's a good boy!' he said encouragingly. 'You'll be grand when you get that up.'

Begor, I was not grand! Grand was the last thing I was. I gave one unmerciful wail out of me as he steered me back to the pub and put me sitting on the bench near the shawlies. They drew themselves up with an offended air, still sore at the suggestion that they had drunk his pint.

'God help us!' moaned one, looking pityingly at me, 'isn't it the likes of them would be fathers?'

'Mick,' said the publican in alarm, spraying sawdust on my tracks, 'that child isn't supposed to be in here at all. You'd better take him home quick in case a bobby would see him.'

'Merciful God!' whimpered Father, raising his eyes to heaven and clapping his hands silently as he only did when distraught, 'what misfortune was on me? Or what will his mother say? ... If women might stop at home and look after their children themselves!' he added in a snarl for the benefit of the shawlies. 'Are them carriages all gone, Bill?'

'The carriages are finished long ago, Mick,' replied the publican.

'I'll take him home,' Father said despairingly ... 'I'll never bring you out again.' he threatened me. 'Here,' he added, giving me the clean handkerchief from his breast pocket, 'put that over your eye.'

The blood on the handkerchief was the first indication I got that I was cut, and instantly my temple began to throb and I set up another howl.

'Whisht, whisht, whisht!' Father said testily, steering me out the door. 'One'd think you were killed. That's nothing. We'll wash it when we get home.'

'Steady now, old scout!' Crowley said, taking the other side of me. 'You'll be all right in a minute.'

I never met two men who knew less about the effects of drink. The first breath of fresh air and the warmth of the sun made me groggier than ever and I pitched and rolled between wind and tide till Father started to whimper again.

'God Almighty, and the whole road out! What misfortune was on me didn't stop at my work! Can't you walk straight?'

I couldn't. I saw plain enough that, coaxed by the sunlight, every woman old and young in Blarney Lane was leaning over her half-door or sitting on her doorstep. They all stopped gabbling to gape at the strange spectacle of two sober, middle-aged men bringing home a drunken small boy with a cut over his eye. Father, torn between the shamefast desire to get me home as quick as he could, and the neighbourly need to explain that it wasn't his fault, finally halted outside Mrs Roche's. There was a gang of old women outside a door at the opposite side of the road. I didn't like the look of them from the first. They seemed altogether too interested in me. I leaned against the wall of Mrs Roche's cottage with my hands in my trouser pockets, thinking mournfully of poor Mr Dooley in his cold grave on the Curragh, who would never walk down the road again, and, with great feeling, I began to sing a favourite song of Father's.

Though lost to Mononia and cold in the grave
He returns to Kincora no more.

'Wisha, the poor child!' Mrs Roche said. 'Haven't he a lovely voice, God bless him!' That was what I thought myself, so I was the more surprised when Father said 'Whisht!' and raised a threatening finger at me. He didn't seem to realise the appropriateness of the song, so I sang louder than ever. 'Whisht, I tell you!' he snapped, and then tried to work up a smile for Mrs Roche's benefit. 'We're nearly home now. I'll carry you the rest of the way.'

But, drunk and all as I was, I knew better than to be carried home ignominiously like that.

'Now,' I said severely, 'can't you leave me alone? I can walk all right. 'Tis only my head. All I want is a rest.'

'But you can rest at home in bed,' he said viciously, trying to pick me up, and I knew by the flush on his face that he was very vexed.

'Ah, Jasus,' I said crossly, 'what do I want to go home for? Why the hell can't you leave me alone?'

For some reason the gang of old women at the other side of the road thought this very funny. They nearly split their sides over it. A gassy fury began to expand in me at the thought that a fellow couldn't have a drop taken without the whole neighbourhood coming out to make game of him.

'Who are ye laughing at?' I shouted, clenching my fists at them. 'I'll make ye laugh at the other side of yeer faces if ye don't let me pass.'

They seemed to think this funnier still; I had never seen such ill-mannered people.

'Go away, ye bloody bitches!' I said.

'Whisht, whisht, whisht, I tell you!' snarled Father, abandoning all pretence of amusement and dragging me along behind him by the hand. I was maddened by the women's shrieks of laughter. I was maddened by Father's bullying. I tried to dig in my heels but he was too powerful for me, and I could only see the women by looking back over my shoulder.

'Take care or I'll come back and show ye!' I shouted.

'I'll teach ye to let decent people pass. Fitter for ye to stop at home and wash yeer dirty faces.'

'Twill be all over the road,' whimpered Father. 'Never again, never again, not if I lived to be a thousand!'

To this day I don't know whether he was forswearing me or the drink. By way of a song suitable to my heroic mood I bawled 'The Boys of Wexford', as he dragged me in home. Crowley, knowing he was not safe, made off and Father undressed me and put me to bed. I couldn't sleep because of the whirling in my head. It was very unpleasant, and I got sick again. Father came in with a wet cloth and mopped up after me. I lay in a fever, listening to him chopping sticks to start a fire. After that I heard him lay the table. Suddenly the front door banged open and Mother stormed in with Sonny in her arms, not her usual gentle, timid self, but a wild, raging woman. It was clear that she had heard it all from the neighbours.

'Mick Delaney,' she cried hysterically, 'what did you do to my son?'

'Whisht, woman, whisht, whisht!' he hissed, dancing from one foot to the other. 'Do you want the whole road to hear?'

'Ah,' she said with a horrifying laugh, 'the road knows all about it by this time. The road knows the way you filled your unfortunate innocent child with drink to make sport for you and that other rotten, filthy brute.'

'But I gave him no drink,' he shouted, aghast at the horrifying interpretation the neighbours had chosen to give his misfortune.

'He took it while my back was turned. What the hell do you think I am?'

'Ah,' she replied bitterly, 'everyone knows what you are now. God forgive you, wasting our hard-earned few ha'pence on drink, and bringing up your child to be a drunken corner-boy like yourself.'

Then she swept into the bedroom and threw herself on her knees by the bed. She moaned when she saw the gash over my eye. In the kitchen Sonny set up a loud bawl on his own, and a moment later Father appeared in the bedroom door with his cap over his eyes, wearing an expression of the most intense self-pity.

'That's a nice way to talk to me after all I went through,' he whined. 'That's a nice accusation, that I was drinking. Not one drop of drink crossed my lips the whole day. How could it when he drank it all? I'm the one that ought to be pitied, with my day ruined on me, and I after being made a show for the whole road.'

But next morning, when he got up and went out quietly to work with his dinner-basket, Mother threw herself on me in the bed and kissed me. It seemed it was all my doing, and I was being given a holiday till my eye got better.

'My brave little man!' she said with her eyes shining. 'It was God did it you were there. You were his guardian angel.'

The Genius

Some kids are cissies by nature but I was a cissy by conviction.
Mother had told me about geniuses; I wanted to be one and I
could see for myself that fighting, as well as being sinful, was
dangerous. The kids round the Barrack where I lived were always
fighting. Mother said they were savages, that I needed proper
friends, and that once I was old enough to go to school I would
meet them.

My way, when someone wanted to fight and I could not get away,
was to climb on the nearest wall and argue like hell in a shrill voice
about Our Blessed Lord and good manners. This was a way of
attracting attention, and it usually worked because the enemy,
having stared incredulously at me for several minutes, wondering
if he would have time to hammer my head on the pavement
before someone came out to him, yelled something like 'blooming cissy' and went away in disgust. I didn't like being called a
cissy but I preferred it to fighting. I felt very like one of those poor
mongrels who slunk through our neighbourhood and took to
their heels when anyone came near them, and I always tried to
make friends with them.

I toyed with games, and enjoyed kicking a ball gently before me
along the pavement till I discovered that any boy who joined me
grew violent and started to shoulder me out of the way. I
preferred little girls because they didn't fight so much, but
otherwise I found them insipid and lacking in any solid basis of
information. The only women I cared for were grownups, and
my most intimate friend was an old washerwoman called Miss
Cooney who had been in the lunatic asylum and was very
religious. It was she who had told me all about dogs. She would
run a mile after anyone she saw hurting an animal, and even went

to the police about them, but the police knew she was mad and paid no attention.

She was a sad-looking woman with grey hair, high cheekbones and toothless gums. While she ironed, I would sit for hours in the hot, steaming, damp kitchen, turning over the pages of her religious books. She was fond of me too, and told me she was sure I would be a priest. I agreed that I might be a bishop, but she didn't seem to think so highly of bishops. I told her there were so many other things I might be that I couldn't make up my mind, but she only smiled at this. Miss Cooney thought there was only one thing a genius could be and that was a priest.

On the whole I thought an explorer was what I would be. Our house was in a square between two roads, one terraced above the other, and I could leave home, follow the upper road for a mile past the Barrack, turn left on any of the intervening roads and lanes, and return almost without leaving the pavement. It was astonishing what valuable information you could pick up on a trip like that. When I came home I wrote down my adventures in a book called *The Voyages of Johnson Martin*, 'with many Maps and Illustrations, Irishtown University Press, 3s. 6d. nett'. I was also compiling *The Irishtown University Song Book for Use in Schools and Institutions by Johnson Martin*, which had the words and music of my favourite songs. I could not read music yet but I copied it from anything that came handy, preferring staff to solfa because it looked better on the page. But I still wasn't sure what I would be. All I knew was that I intended to be famous and have a statue put up to me near that of Father Matthew, in Patrick Street. Father Matthew was called the Apostle of Temperance, but I didn't think much of temperance. So far our town hadn't a proper genius and I intended to supply the deficiency.

But my work continued to bring home to me the great gaps in my knowledge. Mother understood my difficulty and worried herself endlessly finding answers to my questions, but neither she nor Miss Cooney had a great store of the sort of information I needed, and Father was more a hindrance than a help. He was talkative enough about subjects that interested himself but they did not greatly interest me. 'Ballybeg,' he would say brightly. 'Market town. Population 648. Nearest station, Rathkeale.' He was also forthcoming enough about other things, but later, Mother would take me aside and explain that he was only joking again. This made me mad, because I never knew when he was joking and when he wasn't.

I can see now, of course, that he didn't really like me. It was not the poor man's fault. He had never expected to be the father of a genius and it filled him with forebodings. He looked round him at all his contemporaries who had normal, bloodthirsty, illiterate children, and shuddered at the thought that I would never be good for anything but being a genius. To give him his due, it wasn't himself he worried about, but there had never been anything like it in the family before and he dreaded the shame of it. He would come in from the front door with his cap over his eyes and his hands in his trouser pockets and stare moodily at me while I sat at the kitchen table, surrounded by papers, producing fresh maps and illustrations for my book of voyages, or copying the music of 'The Minstrel Boy'.

'Why can't you go out and play with the Horgans?' he would ask wheedlingly, trying to make it sound attractive.

'I don't like the Horgans, Daddy,' I would reply politely.

'But what's wrong with them?' he would ask testily. 'They're fine manly young fellows.'

'They're always fighting, Daddy.'

'And what harm is fighting? Can't you fight them back?'

'I don't like fighting, Daddy, thank you,' I would say, still with perfect politeness.

'The dear knows, the child is right,' Mother would say, coming to my defence. 'I don't know what sort those children are.'

'Ah, you have him as bad as yourself,' Father would snort, and stalk to the front door again, to scald his heart with thoughts of the nice natural son he might have had if only he hadn't married the wrong woman. Granny had always said Mother was the wrong woman for him and now she was being proved right.

She was being proved so right that the poor man couldn't keep his eyes off me, waiting for the insanity to break out in me. One of the things he didn't like was my Opera House. The Opera House was a cardboard box I had mounted on two chairs in the dark hallway. It had a proscenium cut in it, and I had painted some back-drops of mountain and sea, with wings that represented trees and rocks. The characters were pictures cut out, mounted and coloured, and moved on bits of stick. It was lit with candles, for which I had made coloured screens, greased so that they were transparent, and I made up operas from story-books and bits of songs. I was singing a passionate duet for two of the characters while twiddling the screens to produce the effect of moonlight when one of the screens caught fire and everything went up in a mass of flames. I screamed and Father came out to stamp out the blaze, and he cursed me till even Mother lost her temper with him and told him he was worse than six children, after which he wouldn't speak to her for a week.

Another time I was so impressed with a lame teacher I knew that I decided to have a lame leg myself, and there was hell in the home for days because Mother had no difficulty at all in seeing that my foot was already out of shape while Father only looked at it and sniffed contemptuously. I was furious with him, and Mother decided he wasn't much better than a monster They quarrelled for days over that until it became quite an embarrassment to me because, though I was bored stiff with limping, I felt I should be letting her down by getting better. When I went down the Square, lurching from side to side, Father stood at the gate, looking after me with a malicious knowing smile, and when I had discarded my limp, the way he mocked Mother was positively disgusting.

2

As I say, they squabbled endlessly about what I should be told. Father was for telling me nothing.

'But, Mick,' Mother would say earnestly, 'the child must learn.'

'He'll learn soon enough when he goes to school,' he snarled. 'Why do you be always at him, putting ideas into his head? Isn't he bad enough? I'd sooner the boy would grow up a bit natural.' But either Mother didn't like children to be natural or she thought I was natural enough as I was. Women, of course, don't object to geniuses half as much as men do. I suppose they find them a relief.

Now one of the things I wanted badly to know was where babies came from, but this was something that no one seemed to be able to explain to me. When I asked Mother she got upset and talked about birds and flowers, and I decided that if she had ever known she must have forgotten it and was ashamed to say so. Miss Cooney only smiled wistfully when I asked her and said, 'You'll know all about it soon enough, child.'

'But, Miss Cooney,' I said with great dignity, 'I have to know now. It's for my work, you see.'

'Keep your innocence while you can, child,' she said in the same tone. 'Soon enough the world will rob you of it, and once 'tis gone 'tis gone for ever.'

But whatever the world wanted to rob me of, it was welcome to it from my point of view, if only I could get a few facts to work on. I appealed to Father and he told me that babies were dropped out of aeroplanes and if you caught one you could keep it. 'By parachute?' I asked, but he only looked pained and said, 'Oh, no, you don't want to begin by spoiling them.' Afterwards, Mother took me aside again and explained that he was only joking. I went quite dotty with rage and told her that one of these days be would go too far with his jokes.

All the same, it was a great worry to Mother. It wasn't every mother who had a genius for a son, and she dreaded that she might be wronging me. She suggested timidly to Father that he should tell me something about it and he danced with rage. I heard them because I was supposed to be playing with the Opera House upstairs at the time. He said she was going out of her mind, and that she was driving me out of my mind at the same time. She was very upset because she had considerable respect for his judgement.

At the same time when it was a matter of duty she could be very, very obstinate. It was a heavy responsibility, and she disliked it intensely a deeply pious woman who never mentioned the subject at all to anybody if she could avoid it but it had to be done. She took an awful long time over it it was a summer day, and we were sitting on the bank of a stream in the Glen but at last I managed to detach the fact that mummies had an engine in their tummies and daddies had a starting-handle that made it work, and once it started it went on until it made a baby. That certainly explained an awful lot of things I had not understood up to this for instance, why fathers were necessary and why Mother had buffers on her chest while Father had none. It made her almost as interesting as a locomotive, and for days I went round deploring my own rotten luck that I wasn't a girl and couldn't have an engine and buffers of my own instead of a measly old starting-handle like Father.

Soon afterwards I went to school and disliked it intensely. I was too small to be moved up to the big boys and the other 'infants' were still at the stage of spelling 'cat' and 'dog'. I tried to tell the old teacher about my work, but she only smiled and said, 'Hush, Larry!' I hated being told to hush. Father was always saying it to me.

One day I was standing at the playground gate, feeling very lonely and dissatisfied, when a tall girl from the Senior Girls' school spoke to me. She was a girl with a plump, dark face and black pigtails.

'What's your name, little boy?' she asked.

I told her.

'Is this your first time at school?' she asked.

'Yes.'

'And do you like it?'

'No, I hate it,' I replied gravely. 'The children can't spell and the old woman talked too much.'

Then I talked myself for a change and she listened attentively while I told her about myself, my voyages, my books and the time of the trains from all the city stations As she seemed so interested I told her I would meet her after school and tell her some more. I was as good as my word. When I had eaten my lunch, instead of going on further voyages I went back to the Girls' School and waited for her to come out. She seemed pleased to see me because she took my hand and brought me home with her. She lived up Gardiner's Hill, a steep, demure suburban road with trees that overhung the walls at either side. She lived in a small house on top of the hill and was one of a family of three girls. Her little brother, John Joe, had been killed the previous year by a car. 'Look at what I brought home with me!' she said when we went into the kitchen, and her mother, a tall, thin woman made a great fuss of me and wanted me to have my dinner with Una. That was the girl's name. I didn't take anything, but while she ate I sat by the range and told her mother about myself as well. She seemed to like it as much as Una, and when dinner was over Una took me out in the fields behind the house for a walk. When I went home at teatime, Mother was delighted.

'Ah,' she said, 'I knew you wouldn't be long making nice friends at school. It's about time for you, the dear knows.'

I felt much the same about it, and every fine day at three I waited for Una outside the school. When it rained and Mother would not let me out I was miserable.

One day while I was waiting for her there were two senior girls outside the gate.

'Your girl isn't out yet, Larry,' said one with a giggle.

'And do you mean to tell me Larry has a girl?' the other asked with a shocked air.

'Oh, yes,' said the first. 'Una Dwyer is Larry's girl. He goes with Una, don't you, Larry?'

I replied politely that I did, but in fact I was seriously alarmed. I had not realised that Una would be considered my girl. It had never happened to me before, and I had not understood that my waiting for her would be regarded in such a grave light. Now, I think the girls were probably right anyhow, for that is always the way it has happened to me. A woman has only to shut up and let me talk long enough for me to fall head and ears in love with her. But then I did not recognise the symptoms. All I knew was that going with somebody meant you intended to marry them. I had always planned on marrying Mother; now it seemed as if I was expected to marry someone else, and I wasn't sure if I should like it or if, like football, it would prove to be one of those games that two people could not play without pushing.

A couple of weeks later I went to a party at Una's house. By this time it was almost as much mine as theirs. All the girls liked me and Mrs Dwyer talked to me by the hour. I saw nothing peculiar about this except a proper appreciation of geniuses. Una had warned me that I should be expected to sing, so I was ready for the occasion. I sang the Gregorian *Credo*, and some of the little girls laughed, but Mrs Dwyer only looked at me fondly.

'I suppose you'll be a priest when you grow up, Larry?' she asked.

'No, Mrs Dwyer,' I replied firmly. 'As a matter of fact, I intend to be a composer. Priests can't marry, you see, and I want to get married.'

That seemed to surprise her quite a bit. I was quite prepared to continue discussing my plans for the future, but all the children talked together. I was used to planning discussions so that they went on for a long time, but I found that whenever I began one in the Dwyers', it was immediately interrupted so that I found it hard to concentrate. Besides, all the children shouted, and Mrs Dwyer, for all her gentleness, shouted with them and at them. At first, I was somewhat alarmed, but I soon saw that they meant no particular harm, and when the party ended I was jumping up and down on the sofa, shrieking louder than anyone while Una, in hysterics of giggling, encouraged me. She seemed to think I was the funniest thing ever.

It was a moonlit November night, and lights were burning in the little cottages along the road when Una brought me home. On the road outside she stopped uncertainly and said, 'This is where little John Joe was killed.' There was nothing remarkable about the spot, and I saw no chance of acquiring any useful information.

'Was it a Ford or a Morris?' I asked, more out of politeness than anything else.

'I don't know,' she replied with smouldering anger. 'It was Donegan's old car. They can never look where they're going, the old shows!'

'Our Lord probably wanted him,' I said perfunctorily.

'I dare say He did,' Una replied, though she showed no particular conviction. 'That old fool, Donegan I could kill him whenever I think of it.'

'You should get your mother to make you another,' I suggested helpfully. 'Make me a what?' Una exclaimed in consternation.

'Make you another brother,' I repeated earnestly. 'It's quite easy, really. She has an engine in her tummy, and all your daddy has to do is to start it with his starting-handle.'

'Cripes!' Una said, and clapped her hand over her mouth in an explosion of giggles. 'Imagine me telling her that!'

'But it's true, Una,' I said obstinately. 'It only takes nine months.' 'She could make you another little brother by next summer.'

'Oh, Jay!' exclaimed Una in another fit of giggles. 'Who told you all that?'

'Mummy did. Didn't your mother tell you?'

'Oh, she says you buy them from Nurse Dally,' said Una, and began to giggle again.

'I wouldn't really believe that,' I said with as much dignity as I could muster.

But the truth was I felt I had made a fool of myself again. I realised now that I had never been convinced by Mother's explanation. It was too simple. If there was anything that woman could get wrong she did so without fail. And it upset me, because for the first time I found myself wanting to make a really good impression. The Dwyers had managed to convince me that whatever else I wanted to be I did not want to be a priest. I didn't even want to be an explorer, a career which would take me away for long periods from my wife and family. I was prepared to be a composer and nothing but a composer.

That night in bed I sounded Mother on the subject of marriage. I tried to be tactful because it had always been agreed between us that I should marry her and I did not wish her to see that my feelings had changed.

'Mummy,' I asked, 'if a gentleman asks a lady to marry him, what does he say?'

'Oh,' she replied shortly, 'some of them say a lot. They say more than they mean.'

She was so irritable that I guessed she had divined my secret and I felt really sorry for her.

'If a gentleman said, "Excuse me, will you marry me?" would that be all right?' I persisted.

'Ah, well, he'd have to tell her first that he was fond of her,' said Mother who, no matter what she felt, could never bring herself to deceive me on any major issue.

But about the other matter I saw that it was hopeless to ask her any more. For days I made the most pertinacious inquiries at school and received some startling information. One boy had actually come floating down on a snowflake, wearing a bright blue dress, but to his chagrin and mine, the dress had been given away to a poor child in the North Main Street. I grieved long and deeply over this wanton destruction of evidence. The balance of opinion favoured Mrs Dwyer's solution, but of the theory of engines and starting-handles no one in the school had ever heard. That theory might have been all right when Mother was a girl but it was now definitely out of fashion.

And because of it I had been exposed to ridicule before the family whose good opinion I valued most. It was hard enough to keep up my dignity with a girl who was doing algebra while I hadn't got beyond long division without falling into childish errors that made her laugh. That is another thing I still cannot stand, being made fun of by women. Once they begin on it they never stop. Once when we were going up Gardiner's Hill together after school she stopped to look at a baby in a pram. The baby grinned at her and she gave him her finger to suck. He waved his fists and sucked like mad, and she went off into giggles again.

'I suppose that was another engine?' she said.

Four times at least she mentioned my silliness, twice in front of other girls and each time, though I pretended to ignore it, I was pierced to the heart. It made me determined not to be exposed again. Once Mother asked Una and her younger sister, Joan, to tea, and all the time I was in an agony of self-consciousness, dreading what she would say next. I felt that a woman who had said such things about babies was capable of anything. Then the talk turned on the death of little John Joe, and it all flowed back into my mind on a wave of mortification. I made two efforts to change the conversation, but Mother returned to it. She was full of pity for the Dwyers, full of sympathy for the little boy and had almost reduced herself to tears. Finally I got up and ordered Una and Joan to play with me. Then Mother got angry.

'For goodness' sake, Larry, let the children finish their tea!' she snapped.

'It's all right, Mrs Delaney,' Una said good-naturedly. 'I'll go with him.'

'Nonsense, Una' Mother said sharply. 'Finish your tea and go on with what you were saying. It's a wonder to me your poor mother didn't go out of her mind. How can they let people like that drive cars?'

At this I set up a loud wail. At any moment now I felt she was going to get on to babies and advise Una about what her mother ought to do.

'Will you behave yourself, Larry?' Mother said in a quivering voice. 'Or what's come over you in the past few weeks? You used to have such nice manners, and now look at you! A little corner-boy I'm ashamed of you!'

How could she know what had come over me? How could she realise that I was imagining the family circle in the Dwyers' house and Una, between fits of laughter, describing my old-fashioned mother who still talked about babies coming out of people's stomachs? It must have been real love, for I have never known true love in which I wasn't ashamed of Mother.

And she knew it and was hurt. I still enjoyed going home with Una in the afternoons and while she ate her dinner, I sat at the piano and pretended to play my own compositions, but whenever she called at our house for me I grabbed her by the hand and tried to drag her away so that she and Mother shouldn't start talking.

'Ah, I'm disgusted with you,' Mother said one day. 'One would think you were ashamed of me in front of that little girl. I'll engage she doesn't treat her mother like that.'

Then one day I was waiting for Una at the school gate as usual. Another boy was waiting there as well one of the seniors. When he heard the screams of the school breaking up he strolled away and stationed himself at the foot of the hill by the crossroads. Then Una herself came rushing out in her wide-brimmed felt hat, swinging her satchel, and approached me with a conspiratorial air.

'Oh, Larry, guess what's happened!' she whispered. 'I can't bring you home with me today. I'll come down and see you during the week though. Will that do?'

'Yes, thank you,' I said in a dead cold voice. Even at the most tragic moment of my life I could be nothing but polite. I watched her scamper down the hill to where the big boy was waiting. He looked over his shoulder with a grin, and then the two of them went off together.

Instead of following them I went back up the hill alone and stood leaning over the quarry wall, looking at the roadway and the valley of the city beneath me. I knew this was the end. I was too young to marry Una. I didn't know where babies came from and I didn't understand algebra. The fellow she had gone home with probably knew everything about both. I was full of gloom and revengeful thoughts. I, who had considered it sinful and dangerous to fight, was now regretting that I hadn't gone after him to batter his teeth in and jump on his face; It wouldn't even have mattered to me that I was too young and weak and that he would have done all the battering. I saw that love was a game that two people couldn't play at without pushing, just like football.

I went home and, without saying a word, took out the work I had been neglecting so long. That too seemed to have lost its appeal. Moodily I ruled five lines and began to trace the difficult sign of the treble clef.

'Didn't you see Una, Larry?' Mother asked in surprise, looking up from her sewing.

'No, Mummy,' I said, too full for speech.

'Wisha, 'twasn't a falling-out ye had?' she asked in dismay, coming towards me. I put my head on my hands and sobbed. 'Wisha, never mind, childeen!' she murmured, running her hand through my hair. 'She was a bit old for you. You reminded her of her little brother that was killed, of course that was why. You'll soon make new friends, take my word for it.'

But I did not believe her. That evening there was no comfort for me. My great work meant nothing to me and I knew it was all I would ever have. For all the difference it made I might as well become a priest. I felt it was a poor, sad, lonesome thing being nothing but a genius.

Christmas Morning

I never really liked my brother, Sonny. From the time he was a baby he was always the mother's pet and always chasing her to tell her what mischief I was up to. Mind you, I was usually up to something. Until I was nine or ten I was never much good at school, and I really believe it was to spite me that he was so smart at his books. He seemed to know by instinct that this was what Mother had set her heart on, and you might almost say he spelt himself into her favour.

'Mummy,' he'd say, 'will I call Larry in to his t-e-a?' or: 'Mummy, the k-e-t-e-l is boiling,' and, of course, when he was wrong she'd correct him, and next time he'd have it right and there would be no standing him. 'Mummy,' he'd say, 'aren't I a good speller?' Cripes, we could all be good spellers if we went on like that!

Mind you, it wasn't that I was stupid. Far from it. I was just restless and not able to fix my mind for long on any one thing. I'd do the lessons for the year before, or the lessons for the year after: what I couldn't stand were the lessons we were supposed to be doing at the time. In the evenings I used to go out and play with the Doherty gang. Not, again, that I was rough, but I liked the excitement, and for the life of me I couldn't see what attracted Mother about education.

'Can't you do your lessons first and play after?' she'd say, getting white with indignation. 'You ought to be ashamed of yourself that your baby brother can read better than you.'

She didn't seem to understand that I wasn't, because there didn't seem to me to be anything particularly praiseworthy about reading, and it struck me as an occupation better suited to a sissy kid like Sonny.

'The dear knows what will become of you,' she'd say. 'If only you'd stick to your books you might be something good like a clerk or an engineer.'

'I'll be a clerk, Mummy,' Sonny would say smugly.

'Who wants to be an old clerk?' I'd say, just to annoy him. 'I'm going to be a soldier.'

'The dear knows, I'm afraid that's all you'll ever be fit for,' she would add with a sigh.

I couldn't help feeling at times that she wasn't all there. As if there was anything better a fellow could be!

Coming on to Christmas, with the days getting shorter and the shopping crowds bigger, I began to think of all the things I might get from Santa Claus. The Dohertys said there was no Santa Claus, only what your father and mother gave you, but the Dohertys were a rough class of children you wouldn't expect Santa to come to anyway. I was rooting round for whatever information I could pick up about him, but there didn't seem to be much. I was no hand with a pen, but if a letter would do any good I was ready to chance writing to him. I had plenty of initiative and was always writing off for free samples and prospectuses.

'Ah, I don't know will he come at all this year,' Mother said with a worried air. 'He has enough to do looking after steady boys who mind their lessons without bothering about the rest.'

'He only comes to good spellers, Mummy,' said Sonny. 'Isn't that right?'

'He comes to any little boy who does his best, whether he's a good speller or not,' Mother said firmly.

Well, I did my best. God knows I did! It wasn't my fault if, four days before the holidays, Flogger Dawley gave us sums we couldn't do, and Peter Doherty and myself had to go on the lang. It wasn't for the love of it, for, take it from me, December is no month for mitching, and we spent most of our time sheltering from the rain in a store on the quays. The only mistake we made was imagining we could keep it up till the holidays without being spotted. That showed real lack of foresight.

Of course, Flogger Dawley noticed and sent home word to know what was keeping me. When I came in on the third day the mother gave me a look I'll never forget, and said: 'Your dinner is there.' She was too full to talk. When I tried to explain to her about Flogger Dawley and the sums she brushed it aside and said: 'You have no word.' I saw then it wasn't the langing she minded but the lies, though I still didn't see how you could lang without lying. She didn't speak to me for days. And even then I couldn't make out what she saw in education, or why she wouldn't let me grow up naturally like anyone else.

To make things worse, it stuffed Sonny up more than ever. He had the air of one saying: 'I don't know what they'd do without me in this blooming house.' He stood at the front door, leaning against the jamb with his hands in his trouser pockets, trying to make himself look like Father, and shouted to the other kids so that he could be heard all over the road.

'Larry isn't left go out. He went on the lang with Peter Doherty and me mother isn't talking to him.'

And at night, when we were in bed, he kept it up. 'Santa Claus won't bring you anything this year, aha!'

'Of course he will,' I said.

'How do you know?'

'Why wouldn't he?'

'Because you went on the lang with Doherty. I wouldn't play with them Doherty fellows.'

'You wouldn't be left'

'I wouldn't play with them. They're no class. They had the bobbies up to the house.'

'And how would Santa know I was on the lang with Peter Doherty?' I growled, losing patience with the little prig.

'Of course he'd know. Mummy would tell him.'

'And how could Mummy tell him and he up at the North Pole? Poor Ireland, she's rearing them yet 'Tis easy seen you're only an old baby.'

'I'm not a baby, and I can spell better than you, and Santa won't bring you anything.'

'We'll see whether he will or not,' I said sarcastically, doing the old man on him.

But, to tell the God's truth, the old man was only bluff. You could never tell what powers these superhuman chaps would have of knowing what you were up to. And I had a bad conscience about the langing because I'd never before seen the mother like that. That was the night I decided that the only sensible thing to do was to see Santa myself and explain to him. Being a man, he'd probably understand. In those days I was a good-looking kid and had a way with me when I liked. I had only to smile nicely at one old gent on the North Mall to get a penny from him, and I felt if only I could get Santa by himself I could do the same with him and maybe get something worthwhile from him. I wanted a model railway: I was sick of Ludo and Snakes-and-Ladders.

I started to practise lying awake, counting five hundred and then a thousand, and trying to hear first eleven, then midnight, from Shandon. I felt sure Santa would be round by midnight, seeing that he'd be coming from the north, and would have the whole of the south side to do afterwards. In some ways I was very farsighted. The only trouble was the things I was farsighted about.

I was so wrapped up in my own calculations that I had little attention to spare for Mother's difficulties. Sonny and I used to go to town with her, and while she was shopping we stood outside a toyshop in the North Main Street, arguing about what we'd like for Christmas.

On Christmas Eve when Father came home from work and gave her the housekeeping money, she stood looking at it doubtfully while her face grew white.

'Well?' he snapped, getting angry. 'What's wrong with that?'

'What's wrong with it?' she muttered. 'On Christmas Eve!'

'Well,' he asked truculently, sticking his hands in his trouser pockets as though to guard what was left, 'do you think I get more because it's Christmas?'

'Lord God,' she muttered distractedly. 'And not a bit of cake in the house, nor a candle, nor anything!'

'All right,' he shouted, beginning to stamp. 'How much will the candle be?'

'Ah, for pity's sake,' she cried, 'will you give me the money and not argue like that before the children? Do you think I'll leave them with nothing on the one day of the year?'

'Bad luck to you and your children!' he snarled. 'Am I to be slaving from one year's end to another for you to be throwing it away on toys? Here,' he added, tossing two half-crowns on the table, 'that's all you're going to get, so make the most of it.'

'I suppose the publicans will get the rest,' she said bitterly.

Later she went into town, but did not bring us with her, and returned with a lot of parcels, including the Christmas candle. We waited for Father to come home to his tea, but he didn't, so we had our own tea and a slice of Christmas cake each, and then Mother put Sonny on a chair with the holy-water stoup to sprinkle the candle, and when he lit it she said: 'The light of heaven to our souls.' I could see she was upset because Father wasn't in it should be the oldest and youngest. When we hung up our stockings at bedtime he was still out.

Then began the hardest couple of hours I ever put in. I was mad with sleep but afraid of losing the model railway, so I lay for a while, making up things to say to Santa when he came. They varied in tone from frivolous to grave, for some old gents like kids to be modest and well spoken, while others prefer them with spirit. When I had rehearsed them all I tried to wake Sonny to keep me company, but that kid slept like the dead.

Eleven struck from Shandon, and soon after I heard the latch, but it was only Father coming home.

'Hello, little girl,' he said, letting on to be surprised at finding Mother waiting for him, and then broke into a self-conscious giggle. 'What have you up so late?'

'Do you want your supper?' she asked shortly.

'Ah, no, no,' he replied. 'I had a bit of pig's cheek at Daneen's on my way up.' (Daneen was my uncle.) 'I'm very fond of a bit of pig's cheek . . . My goodness, is it that late?' he exclaimed, letting on to be astonished. 'If I knew that I'd have gone to the North Chapel for midnight Mass. I'd like to hear the *Adeste* again.

That's a hymn I'm very fond of a most touching hymn.' Then he began to hum it falsetto.

Adeste fideles
Solus domus dagus.

Father was very fond of Latin hymns, particularly when he had a drop in, but as he had no notion of the words he made them up as he went along, and this always drove Mother mad.

'Ah, you disgust me!' she said in a scalded voice, and closed the room door behind her. Father laughed as if he thought it a great joke; and he struck a match to light his pipe and for a while puffed at it noisily. The light under the door dimmed and went out but he continued to sing emotionally.

Dixie medearo
Tutum tonum tandum
Venite adoremus.

He had it all wrong but the effect was the same on me. To save my life I couldn't keep awake.

Coming on to dawn, I woke with the feeling that something dreadful had happened. The whole house was quiet, and the little bedroom that looked out on the foot and a half of back yard was pitch-dark. It was only when I glanced at the window that I saw how all the silver had drained out of the sky. I jumped out of bed to feel my stocking, well knowing that the worst had happened. Santa had come while I was asleep, and gone away with an entirely false impression of me, because all he had left me was some sort of book, folded up, a pen and pencil, and a tuppenny bag of sweets. Not even Snakes-and-Ladders! For a while I was too stunned even to think. A fellow who was able to drive over rooftops and climb down chimneys without getting stuck God, wouldn't you think he'd know better?

Then I began to wonder what that foxy boy, Sonny, had. I went to his side of the bed and felt his stocking. For all his spelling and sucking-up he hadn't done so much better, because, apart from a bag of sweets like mine, all Santa had left him was a popgun, one that fired a cork on a piece of string and which you could get in any huxter's shop for sixpence.

All the same, the fact remained that it was a gun, and a gun was better than a book any day of the week. The Dohertys had a gang, and the gang fought the Strawberry Lane kids who tried to play football on our road. That gun would be very useful to me in many ways, while it would be lost on Sonny who wouldn't be let play with the gang, even if he wanted to.

Then I got the inspiration, as it seemed to me, direct from heaven. Suppose I took the gun and gave Sonny the book! Sonny would never be any good in the gang: he was fond of spelling, and a studious child like him could learn a lot of spellings from a book like mine. As he hadn't seen Santa any more than I had, what he hadn't seen wouldn't grieve him. I was doing no harm to anyone; in fact, if Sonny only knew, I was doing him a good turn which he might have cause to thank me for later. That was one thing I was always keen on; doing good turns. Perhaps this was Santa's intention the whole time and he had merely become confused between us. It was a mistake that might happen to anyone. So I put the book, the pencil, and the pen into Sonny's stocking and the popgun into my own, and returned to bed and slept again. As I say, in those days I had plenty of initiative.

It was Sonny who woke me, shaking me to tell me that Santa had come and left me a gun. I let on to be surprised and rather disappointed in the gun, and to divert his mind from it made him show me his picture book, and cracked it up to the skies.

As I knew, that kid was prepared to believe anything, and nothing would do him then but to take the presents in to show Father and Mother. This was a bad moment for me. After the way she had behaved about the langing, I distrusted Mother, though I had the consolation of believing that the only person who could contradict me was now somewhere up by the North Pole. That gave me a certain confidence, so Sonny and I burst in with our presents, shouting: 'Look what Santa Claus brought!'

Father and Mother woke, and Mother smiled, but only for an instant. As she looked at me her face changed. I knew that look; I knew it only too well. It was the same she had worn the day I came home from langing, when she said I had no word.

'Larry,' she said in a low voice, 'where did you get that gun?'

'Santa left it in my stocking, Mummy,' I said, trying to put on an injured air, though it baffled me how she guessed that he hadn't. 'He did, honest.'

'You stole it from that poor child's stocking while he was asleep,' she said, her voice quivering with indignation. 'Larry, Larry, how could you be so mean?'

'Now, now, now,' Father said deprecatingly, ''tis Christmas morning.'

'Ah,' she said with real passion, 'it's easy it comes to you. Do you think I want my son to grow up a liar and a thief?'

'Ah, what thief, woman?' he said testily. 'Have sense, can't you?' He was as cross if you interrupted him in his benevolent moods as if they were of the other sort, and this one was probably exacerbated by a feeling of guilt for his behaviour of the night before. 'Here, Larry,' he said, reaching out for the money on the bedside table, 'here's sixpence for you and one for Sonny. Mind you don't lose it now!'

But I looked at Mother and saw what was in her eyes. I burst out crying, threw the popgun on the floor, and ran bawling out of the house before anyone on the road was awake. I rushed up the lane beside the house and threw myself on the wet grass.

I understood it all, and it was almost more than I could bear; that there was no Santa Claus, as the Dohertys said, only Mother trying to scrape together a few coppers from the housekeeping; that Father was mean and common and a drunkard, and that she had been relying on me to raise her out of the misery of the life she was leading. And I knew that the look in her eyes was the fear that, like my father, I should turn out to be mean and common and a drunkard.

The Man of the World

When I was a kid there were no such things as holidays for me and my likes, and I have no feeling of grievance about it because in the way of kids I simply invented them, which was much more satisfactory. One year, my summer holiday was a couple of nights I spent at the house of a friend called Jimmy Leary, who lived at the other side of the road from us. His parents sometimes went away for a couple of days to visit a sick relative in Bantry, and he was given permission to have a friend in to keep him company. I took my holiday with the greatest seriousness, insisted on the loan of Father's old travelling-bag and dragged it myself down our lane past the neighbours standing at their doors.

'Are you off somewhere, Larry?' asked one.

'Yes, Mrs Rooney,' I said with great pride. 'Off for my holidays to the Learys.'

'Wisha, aren't you very lucky?' she said with amusement.

'Lucky' seemed an absurd description of my good fortune. The Learys' house was a big one with a high flight of steps up to the front door which was always kept shut. They had a piano in the front room, a pair of binoculars on a table near the window and a toilet on the stairs that seemed to me to be the last word in elegance and immodesty. We brought the binoculars up to the bedroom with us. From the window you could see the whole road up and down, from the quarry at its foot with the tiny houses perched on top of it to the open fields at the other end, where the last gas lamp rose against the sky. Each morning I was up with the first light, leaning out of the window in my nightshirt and watching through the glasses all the mysterious figures you never saw from our lane: policemen, railwaymen and farmers on their way to market.

I admired Jimmy almost as much as I admired his house, and for much the same reasons. He was a year older than I; was well mannered and well dressed, and would not associate with most of the kids on the road at all. He had a way when any of them joined us of resting against a wall with his hands in his trouser pockets and listening to them with a sort of wellbred smile, a knowing smile, that seemed to me the height of elegance. And it was not that he was a softy because he was an excellent boxer and wrestler and could easily have held his own with them any time, but he did not wish to. He was superior to them. He was, there is only one word that still describes it for me, sophisticated.

I attributed his sophistication to the piano, the binoculars and the indoor john, and felt that if only I had the same advantages I could have been sophisticated too. I knew I wasn't because I was always being taken in by the world of appearances. I would take a sudden violent liking to some boy, and when I went to his house my admiration would spread to his parents and sisters, and I would think how wonderful it must be to have such a home; but when I told Jimmy he would smile in that knowing way of his and say quietly, 'I believe they had the bailiffs in a few weeks ago,' and even though I didn't know what bailiffs were, bang would go the whole world of appearances and I would realise that once again I had been deceived.

It was the same with fellows and girls. Seeing some bigger chap we knew walking out with a girl for the first time Jimmy would say casually, 'He'd better mind himself: that one is dynamite.' And even though I knew as little of girls who were dynamite as I did of bailiffs, his tone would be sufficient to indicate that I had been taken in by sweet voices and broadbrimmed hats, gaslight and evening smells from gardens.

Forty years later I can still measure the extent of my obsession, for though my own handwriting is almost illegible, I sometimes find myself scribbling idly on a pad in a small, stiff, perfectly legible hand that I recognise with amusement as a reasonably good forgery of Jimmy's. My admiration still lies there somewhere, a fossil in my memory, but Jimmy's knowing smile is something I have never managed to acquire.

And it all goes back to my curiosity about fellows and girls. As I say, I only imagined things about them but Jimmy knew. I was excluded from knowledge by the world of appearances that blinded and deafened me with emotion. The least thing could excite or depress me: the trees in the morning when I went to early Mass, the stained-glass windows in the church, the blue hilly streets at evening with the green flare of the gas lamps, the smells of cooking and perfume even the smell of a cigarette packet that I had picked up from the gutter and crushed to my nose all kept me at this side of the world of appearances while Jimmy, by right of birth or breeding was always at the other. I wanted him to tell me what it was like, but he didn't seem to be able.

Then one evening he was listening to me talk while he leaned against the pillar of his gate, his pale neat hair framing his pale, good-humoured face. My excitability seemed to rouse in him a mixture of amusement and pity.

'Why don't you come over some night the family is away and I'll show you a few things?' he asked lightly.

'What'll you show me, Jimmy?' I asked eagerly.

'Noticed the new couple that's come to live next door?' he asked with a nod in the direction of the house above his own.

'No,' I admitted in disappointment. It wasn't only that I never knew anything, but I never noticed anything either. and when he described the new family that was lodging there, I realised with chagrin that I didn't even know Mrs MacCarthy who owned the house.

'Oh, they're just a newly married couple,' he said. 'They don't know that they can be seen from our house.'

'But how, Jimmy?'

'Don't look up now,' he said with a dreamy smile, while his eyes strayed over my shoulder in the direction of the lane. Wait till you're going away. Their end wall is only a couple of feet from ours. You can see right into the bedroom from our attic.'

'And what do they do, Jimmy?'

'Oh,' he said with a pleasant laugh, 'everything. You really should come.'

'You bet I'll come,' I said, trying to sound tougher than I felt. It wasn't that I saw anything wrong in it. It was rather that, for all my desire to become like Jimmy, I was afraid of what it might do to me.

But it wasn't enough for me to get behind the world of appearances. I had to study the appearances themselves, and for three evenings I stood under the gas lamp at the foot of our lane, across the road from the MacCarthys till I had identified the new lodgers. The husband was the first I spotted, because he came from his work at a regular hour. He was tall, with stiff jet-black hair and a big black guardsman's moustache that somehow failed to conceal the youthfulness and ingenuousness of his face, which was long and lean. Usually he came accompanied by an older man, and stood chatting for a few minutes outside his door; a black-coated, bowler-hatted figure who made large, sweeping gestures with his evening paper and sometimes doubled up in an explosion of loud laughter.

On the third evening I saw his wife, for she had obviously been waiting for him, looking from behind the parlour curtains, and when she saw him she scurried down the steps to join in the conversation. She had thrown an old jacket about her shoulders and stood there, her arms folded as though to protect herself further from the cold wind that blew down the hill from the open country, while her husband rested one hand fondly on her shoulder.

For the first time I began to feel qualms about what I proposed to do. It was one thing to do it to people you didn't know or care about, but for me even to recognise people was to adopt an emotional attitude towards them, and my attitude to this pair was already one of approval. They looked like people who might approve of me too. That night I remained awake, thinking out the terms of an anonymous letter that would put them on their guard till I had worked myself up into a fever of eloquence and indignation.

But I knew only too well that they would recognise the villain of the letter and that the villain would recognise me, so I did not write it. Instead, I gave way to fits of anger and moodiness against my parents. Yet even these were unreal because on Saturday night when Mother made a parcel of my nightshirt I had now become sufficiently self-conscious not to take a bag I nearly broke down. There was something about my own house that night that upset me all over again. Father, with his cap over his eyes, was sitting under the wall-lamp, reading the paper, and Mother, a shawl about her shoulders, was crouched over the fire from her little wickerwork chair, listening, and I realised that they too were part of the world of appearances I was planning to destroy, and as I said goodnight I almost felt that I was saying goodbye to them as well.

But once inside Jimmy's house I did not care so much. It always had that effect on me, of blowing me up to twice the size, as though I were expanding to greet the piano, the binoculars and the indoor toilet. I tried to pick out a tune on the piano with one hand, and Jimmy, having listened with amusement for some time, sat down and played it himself as I felt it should be played, and this too seemed to be part of his superiority.

'I suppose we'd better put in an appearance of going to bed,' he said disdainfully. 'Someone across the road might notice and tell. *They*'re in town, so I don't suppose they'll be back till late.'

We had a glass of milk in the kitchen, went upstairs, undressed and lay down though we put our overcoats beside the bed. Jimmy had a packet of sweets, but insisted on keeping them till later. 'We may need these before we're done,' he said with his knowing smile, and again I admired his orderliness and restraint. We talked in bed for a quarter of an hour; then put out the light, got up again, donned our overcoats and socks and tiptoed upstairs to the attic. Jimmy led the way with an electric torch. He was a fellow who thought of everything. Even in the attic, all was arranged for our vigil. Two trunks had been drawn up to the little window to act as seats, and there were even cushions on them. Looking out, you could at first see nothing but an expanse of blank wall topped with chimney stacks, but gradually you could make out the outline of a single window, eight or ten feet below. Jimmy sat beside me and opened his packet of sweets which he laid between us.

'Of course, we could have stayed in bed till we heard them come in,' he whispered. 'Usually you can hear them at the front door, but they might have come in quietly or we might have fallen asleep. It's always best to make sure.'

'But why don't they draw the blind?' I asked, as my heart began to beat uncomfortably.

'Because there isn't a blind,' he said with a quiet chuckle. 'Old Mrs MacCarthy never had one, and she's not going to put one in for lodgers who may be gone tomorrow. People like that never rest till they get a house of their own.'

I envied him his nonchalance as he sat back with his legs crossed, sucking a sweet just as though he were waiting in the cinema for the show to begin. I was scared by the darkness and the mystery, and by the sounds that came to us from the road with such extraordinary clarity. Besides, of course, it wasn't my house and I didn't feel at home there. At any moment I expected the front door to open and his parents to come in and catch us.

We must have been waiting for half an hour before we heard voices in the roadway, the sound of a key in the latch and then of a door opening and closing softly. Jimmy reached out and touched my arm lightly. 'This is probably our pair,' he whispered. 'We'd better not speak any more in case they might hear us.' I nodded, wishing I had never come. At that moment a faint light became visible in the great expanse of black wall, a faint, yellow stairlight that was just sufficient to silhouette the window frame beneath us. Then suddenly the whole room lit up. The man I had seen in the street stood by the doorway, his hand still on the switch. I could see it all plainly now, an ordinary small, suburban bedroom with flowery wallpaper, a coloured picture of the Sacred Heart over the double bed with the big brass knobs, a wardrobe and a dressing-table.

The man stood there till the woman came in, removing her hat in a single wide gesture and tossing it from her into a corner of the room. He still stood by the door, taking off his tie. Then he struggled with the collar, his head raised and his face set in an agonised expression. His wife kicked off her shoes, sat on a chair by the bed and began to take off her stockings. All the time she seemed to be talking because her head was raised, looking at him, though you couldn't hear a word she said. I glanced at Jimmy. The light from the window below softly illumined his face as he sucked with tranquil enjoyment.

The woman rose as her husband sat on the bed with his back to us and began to take off his shoes and socks in the same slow, agonised way. At one point he held up his left foot and looked at it with what might have been concern. His wife looked at it too for a moment and then swung halfway round as she unbuttoned her skirt. She undressed in swift, jerky movements, twisting and turning and apparently talking all the time. At one moment she looked into the mirror on the dressing-table and touched her cheek lightly. She crouched as she took off her slip, and then pulled her nightdress over her head and finished her undressing beneath it. As she removed her underclothes she seemed to throw them anywhere at all, and I had a strong impression that there was something haphazard and disorderly about her. Her husband was different. Everything he removed seemed to be removed in order and then put carefully where he could find it most readily in the morning. I watched him take out his watch, look at it carefully, wind it and then hang it neatly over the bed.

Then, to my surprise, she knelt by the bed, facing towards the window, glanced up at the picture of the Sacred Heart, made a large hasty Sign of the Cross and then covered her face with her hands and buried her head in the bedclothes. I looked at Jimmy in dismay but he did not seem to be embarrassed by the sight. The husband, his folded trousers in his hand, moved about the room slowly and carefully as though he did not wish to disturb his wife's devotions, and when he pulled on the trousers of his pyjamas he turned away. After that he put on his pyjama jacket, buttoned it carefully and knelt beside her. He, too, glanced respectfully at the picture and crossed himself slowly and reverently, but he did not bury his face and head as she had done. He knelt upright with nothing of the abandonment suggested by her pose, and with an expression that combined reverence and self-respect. It was the expression of an employee who, while admitting that he might have a few little weaknesses like the rest of the staff, prided himself on having deserved well of the management. Women, his slightly complacent air seemed to indicate, had to adopt these emotional attitudes but he spoke to God as one man to another. He finished his prayers before his wife; again he crossed himself slowly, rose and climbed into bed, glancing again at his watch as he did so.

Several minutes passed before she put her hands out before her on the bed, blessed herself in her wide, sweeping way and rose. She crossed the room in a swift movement that almost escaped me, and next moment the light went out, and it was as if the window through which we had watched the scene had disappeared with it by magic till nothing was left but a blank, black wall mounting to the chimney pots.

Jimmy rose slowly and pointed the way out to me with his flashlight. When we got downstairs we put on the bedroom light, and I saw on his face the virtuous and sophisticated air of a collector who has shown you all his treasures in the best possible light. Faced with that look, I could not bring myself to mention the woman at prayer though I felt her image would be impressed on my memory till the day I died. I could not have explained to him how at that moment everything had changed for me, how, beyond us watching the young married couple from ambush, I had felt someone else, watching us, so that at once we ceased to be the observers and became the observed. And the observed in such a humiliating position that nothing I could imagine our victims doing would have been so degrading.

I wanted to pray myself but found I couldn't. Instead, I lay in bed in the darkness, covering my eyes with my hand, and I think that even then I knew that I should never be sophisticated like Jimmy, never be able to put on a knowing smile, because always beyond the world of appearances I would see only eternity watching.

'Sometimes of course, it's better than that,' Jimmy's drowsy voice said from the darkness. 'You shouldn't judge it by tonight.'

The Procession of Life

At last his father had fulfilled his threat. He was locked out. Since his mother died, a year ago, it had been a cause of dire penalties and direr threats, this question of hours. 'Early to bed,' his father quoted, insisting that he should be home by ten o'clock. He, a grown boy of sixteen to be home at ten o'clock like any kid of twelve! He had risked being late a dozen times before, but tonight had cooked it properly. There was the door locked against him, not a light in the house, and a stony ear to all his knockings and whisperings.

By turns he felt miserable and elated. He had tried sleeping in a garden, but that wasn't a success. Then he had wandered aimlessly into the city and been picked up by a policeman. He looked so young and helpless that the policeman wanted to take him to the barracks, but this was not included in his plans for the night. So he promised the policeman that he would go home directly, and no sooner was he out of the policeman's sight, than he doubled down the quay at the opposite side of the bridge. He walked on for at least a mile until he judged himself safe. The quays were lonely and full of shadows, and he sighed with relief when he saw a watchman's fire glowing redly on the waterfront. He went up to it, and said good-night to the watchman, who was an oldish, bearded man with a sour and repulsive face.

He sat in his little sentry-box, smoking his pipe, and looked, thought Larry, for all the world like a priest in the confessional. But he was swathed in coats and scarves, and a second glance made Larry think not of a priest but of some heathen idol; his face was so bronzed above the grey beard and glowed so majestically in the flickering light of the brasier.

Larry didn't like his situation at all, but he felt his only hope was to stick near the watchman. The city smouldering redly between its hills was in some way unfamiliar and frightening. So were the quays all round him. There were shadowy heaps of timber lying outside the range of the watchman's fire, and behind these he imagined all sorts of strange and frightening things. The river made a clucking, lonely sound against the quay wall, and three or four ships, almost entirely in darkness, swayed about close to the farther bank. He heard the noisy return of a party of sailors from across the water, and once two Lascars went past him in the direction of the bridge.

But the watchman did not seem to welcome Larry's company as much as Larry welcomed his. He was openly incredulous when Larry said he had been locked out.

'Locked out?' he asked suspiciously. 'Then why didn't you kick up hell, hush?'

'What's that, sir?' asked Larry, startled.

'Why didn't you bate the door and kick up hell's delights?'

'God, sir, I'd be afraid to do that!'

At this the watchman started blindly from his box, rubbing the sleep from his eyes and swaying about in the heavy fumes of the brasier.

'Afraid?' he exclaimed scornfully.

'A boy of your age to be afraid of his own father? When I was your age I wouldn't let meself be treated like that. I had a girl of me own, and the first time me ould fella' God rest him! tried to stop me going with her I up with the poker, and hit him such a clout over the poll they had to put six stitches in him in the Infirmary after.' Larry shuddered.

'And what did he do then, sir?' he asked innocently.

'What did he do then?' growled the watchman. 'Ech, he was a quiet man after that I tell you! He couldn't look at me after in the light of day but he'd get a reeling in his head.'

'Lord, sir,' said Larry, 'you must have hit him a terrible stroke!'

'Oh, I quietened him,' said the watchman complacently. 'I quietened him sure enough… And there's a big fella' like you now, and you'd let your father bate you, and never rise a hand in your own self-defence?'

'I would, God help me!' said Larry.

'I suppose you never touched a drop of drink in your life?'

'I did not.'

'And you never took a girl out for a walk?'

'I didn't.'

'Had you ever as much as a pipe in your mouth, tell me?'

'I took a couple of pulls out of me father's pipe once,' said Larry brokenly.

'And I was retching until morning.'

'No wonder you're locked out!' said the watchman contemptuously. 'No wonder at all! I think if I'd a son like you 'twould give me all I could do to keep me hands off him. Get out of me sight!'

Terrified at this extraordinary conclusion, Larry retreated to the edge of the circle of light. He dared not go farther.

'Get out of me sight!' said the watchman again.

'You won't send me away now, sir?' asked Larry in despair.

'Won't I?' asked the watchman ironically. 'Won't I just? There's people comes here at every hour of the night, and am I going to have it said I gathered all the young blackguards of the city about me?'

'I'd go mad with lonesomeness,' Larry cried, his voice rising on a note of fear.

'You'll find company enough in the tramp's shelter on the Marina.'

'I won't go, I won't go! I'll dodge behind the timbers if a stranger comes.'

'You'll do nothing of the kind,' the watchman shouted, losing his temper. 'Clear out now and don't let me see your ugly mug again.'

'I won't go!' Larry repeated hysterically, evading him by running round the brasier. 'I'm frightened, I tell you.'

He had plainly heard the sound of quick footsteps coming in his direction, and he was determined that he would stay. The watchman, too, had heard them, and was equally determined that he would go.

'Bad luck to you!' he whispered despairingly, 'What misfortune brought you this way tonight. If you don't go away I'll strangle you and drop your naked body in the river for the fish to ate. Be off with you, you devil's brat!'

He succeeded in chasing Larry for a few yards when the footsteps suddenly stopped and a woman's voice called out:

'Anybody there?'

'I am,' said the watchman, surlily abandoning the chase.

'I thought you were lost,' the woman said, and her voice sounded in Larry's ears like a peal of bells. He came nearer to the brasier on tiptoe so that the watchman would not perceive him.

'Do you want tea?' the watchman asked sourly.

'Well, you are a perfect gentleman,' the woman's voice went on with a laugh.

'Nice way to speak to a lady!'

'Oh, I know the sort of a lady you are!' the watchman grumbled.

'Squinty!' and now her voice sounded caressing. 'Are you really sore because I left you down the other night? I was sorry, Squinty, honest to God I was, but he was a real nice fella' with tons of dough, and he wanted me so bad!'

Larry, fascinated by the mysterious woman, drew nearer and nearer to the circle of light.

'It isn't only the other night,' the watchman snarled. 'It's every night. You can't see a man but you want to go off with him. I warn you, my girl'

But his girl was no longer listening to him.

'Who's that?' she whispered sharply, peering into the shadows where Larry's boyish face was half-hidden.

'Blast you!' shouted the watchman furiously. 'Aren't you gone yet?'

The woman strode across to where Larry stood and caught him by the arm. He tried to draw back, but she pulled him into the light of the brasier.

'I say, kid,' she said, 'aren't you bashful? Let's have a look at you!... Why, he's a real beauty, that's what he is.'

'I'll splinter his beauty for him in wan minit if he don't get out of this!' the watchman cried. 'I'll settle him. He have the heart played out of me this night already.'

'Ah, be quiet, Squinty!' said the woman appeasingly.

'I'll be the death of him!'

'No, you won't... Don't you be afraid of him, kid. He's not as bad as he sounds... Make a drop of tea for him, Squinty, the poor kid's hands are freezing.'

'I won't make tea for him. I have no liquors to spare for young ragamuffins and sleepouts.'

'Aah, do as you're told!' the woman said disgustedly.

'You know there's only two ponnies,' said the watchman, subsiding.

'Well, him and me'll drink out of the one. Won't we kid?'

And with amazing coolness she put him sitting on an improvised bench before the fire, sat close beside him, and drew his hand comfortingly about her slender waist. Larry held it shyly; for the moment he wasn't even certain that he might lawfully hold it at all. He looked at this magical creature in the same shy way. She had a diminutive face, coloured a ghostly white, and crimson lips that looked fine in the firelight. She was perfumed, too, with a scent that he found overpowering and sweet. There was something magical and compelling about her. And stranger than all, the watchman had fallen under her spell. He brewed the tea and poured it out into two ponnies, grumbling to himself the while. 'You *know* he have no right to set down there,' he was saying. 'Nice trouble I'd be getting into if someone came along and seen a ... seen a woman of the streets and a young reformatory school brat settin' be the fire... Eh, me lady? ... Oh, very well, very well... This'll be put a stop to, this can't go on forever... And you think I don't know what you're up to, huh? Hm? No, no, my dear, you can't fool an old soldier like me that way. This'll be put a stop to.

'What are you saying, Squinty?' the woman asked.

'Oh, don't mind me! Don t mind me!' The watchman laughed bitterly. 'I don't count, but all the same this'll be put a stop to... there's your tea!'

He handed her one of the ponnies, then retreated into his watch box with the second. Inside he fumbled in his pockets, removed a little parcel of bread and butter, and tossed her half, which she deftly caught and shared with Larry. Larry had begun to feel that miracles were a very ordinary thing after all.

'Get outside that, kid,' she said kindly to Larry, handing him the ponny of boiling tea. "Twill warm up your insides. What happened you to be out so late? Kissed the girl and lost the tram?'

'Me ould fella' said Larry, sipping and chewing, 'me ould fella' locked me out! Bad luck to him!' he added with a startling new courage.

'Oh, ay, oh, ay!' commented the watchman bitterly from his box. 'That's the way they speaks of their fathers nowadays! No respect for age or anything else. Better fed than taught.'

'Never mind him, darling,' said the woman consolingly. 'He's old-fashioned, that's what he is!'

Then as Larry made a frightened sign to her, she laughed.

'Are you afraid he'll hear me? Oh, Squinty doesn't mind a bit. We're old friends. He know quite well what I think of him don't you, Squinty?' Her voice dropped to a thrilling whisper, and her hand fondled Larry's knee in a way that sent a shiver of pleasure through him. 'Will you come home with me, darling?' she asked, without listening to the watchman's reply.

'Oh, I know, I know,' the latter answered. 'Nice name this place'll be getting with you and all the immoral men and boys of the city making your rondeyvoos here. Sailors … tramps … reformatory school brats … all sorts and conditions. This'll be put a stop to, my lady. Mark my words, this'll be put a stop to. I know what you're saying, I know what you're whispering. It's no use, my dear. You can't deceive me.'

'I was only asking him if he'd e'er a place to stop.'

'And what is it to you if he haven't, my lady?'

'God help us, you wouldn't like your own son to be out here all night, catching his death of cold or maybe dropping asleep and falling stupid in the fire.'

'I wouldn't like me own son to be connaisseuring with the likes of you either.'

'He might meet with worse,' said the woman, bridling up.

'And where would you bring him?'

'Never mind where I'd bring him! I'd bring him a place he'd be welcome in anyway, not like here.'

The watchman suddenly changed his tone, becoming violent, and at the same time conciliatory.

'You wouldn't leave me here lonesome by meself after all you promised me?' he cried.

'I won't remain here to be insulted either.'

'He can stay, he can stay,' said the watchman submissively. 'I won't say a cross word to him.'

'He'd rather go home with me,' said the woman. 'Wouldn't you, darling?'

'I would,' said Larry decisively.

'Don't you go! Don't you go, young fellow!' shouted the watchman. 'She's an immoral woman... Oh, you low creature,' he continued, 'aren't you ashamed of yourself? Leaving me lonesome night after night, and chasing off with any stranger that comes the way. Last time it was the dandy fellow off the Swedish boat, and now it's a common brat that his own father won't leave in.'

'Now, now, don't be snotty!' said the young woman reprovingly. 'It's not becoming to your years. And if you're good maybe I'll come round and see you tomorrow night.'

'You'll say that and not mean a word of it!' exclaimed the watchman. 'Oh, you low creature. You haven't a spark of honour or decency.'

'Come on home, darling, before he loses his temper,' said the woman good-humouredly. She rose and took Larry's hand, and with a loud 'Good-bye' to the watchman, guided him on to the roadway. As she did so there came the sound of heavy footsteps thudding along the wooden jetty. The woman started nervously and pushed Larry before her towards the shadow of the timber. 'Here, kid,' she whispered, 'we'll go round by the timbers and up the Park. Hurry! Hurry! I hear someone coming.'

The steps drew nearer, and suddenly she dropped Larry's hand and crouched back into the shadows. He heard a quick, stifled cry that terrified him.

'Oh, Sacred Heart, he seen me!' she said, and then in a tense, vicious whisper she cried to the unseen, 'May the divil in hell melt and blind you, you clumsy Tipperary lout!'

'Is that you I seen, Molly?' a jovial voice called from the darkness, and a moment later Larry saw the glint of the fire on an array of silver buttons.

'Yes, constable, it's me,' the woman answered, and Larry could scarcely recognise her voice for the moment, it was so unctuous, so caressing. But again came the fierce mutter beside him, 'Bad luck and end to you, y'ould ram, what divil's notion took you to come this way tonight?'

'Are you alone?' the policeman asked, emerging from the shadows.

'No constable,' she sniggered.

'Is there someone with you?'

'Yes, constable … a friend.'

'Oh, a friend, is there? And what's your friend doing out at this hour of the night?'

He strode across to Larry and shook his arm. 'So you're the friend, me young hopeful? And what have you here at this hour of the night, huh?'

'He was seeing me home, constable, and I took a bit of a weakness so we sat here a while with Squinty.'

'Answer me!' thundered the policeman to Larry. 'And don't try to tell any lies. What have you out at this hour?'

'Me Father,' gasped Larry, 'me father locked me out sir.'

'Mmmm. Your father locked you out, did he? Well, I'm thinking it wouldn't do you any harm to lock you in, d'you hear? How would you like that, eh?'

'Bah!' grunted the watchman.

'What did you say, Squinty?'

'I said right, constable. Right every time! If I'd me way with that sort of young fellow I'd make drisheens of his hide.'

'And what about you, Molly?'

'He's a friend of mine, constable,' the woman said ingratiatingly. 'Let him go now and he won't do it again. I'm finding him a place to sleep the poor child is perished with the cold. Leave him to me, constable. I'll look after him for the night.'

'Aisy now, aisy!' the policeman interrupted heavily. 'We're all friends, aren't we?' 'Yes, constable.'

'And we want to do the best we can by one another, don't we?' 'Yes, constable.'

'I've a word to say to you, so I think I'll take your advice and let the boy go. Squinty will keep an eye on him, won't you, Squinty?'

'You may swear I'll keep an eye on him,' the watchman said viciously.

'That's all right then. Are you satisfied now, Molly?'

'Yes, constable,' she said between her teeth.

'The same place?' 'Yes, constable.'

She turned on her heel and went off slowly along the quay. The darkness was thinning. A faint brightness came from above the hill at the other side of the river. The policeman glanced at it and sighed.

'Well, it's a fine day, thanks be to God,' he said. 'I had a quiet night of it, and after this I'll have a grand sleep for myself. Will you try a drop, Squinty?'

'I will then,' said the watchman greedily.

The policeman took a flask from his pocket and drank from it. He handed it to the watchman, who took another swig and gave it back to him. The policeman held it up to the fire. He closed his left eye and whistled brightly for a few moments. 'There's a *taoscán* in it still,' he commented. 'I suppose you don't drink, young fellow?'

'I don't,' said Larry sourly, 'but I'd drink it now if you'd give it to me.'

'I will, I will,' said the policeman laughing. 'And I after taking your girl from you and all. 'Tis the least I might do. But never mind, young fellow. There's plenty more where she came from.'

Larry choked over a mouthful of the neat whiskey and handed back the empty flask. The policeman drew out a packet of cheap cigarettes and held it towards him.

'Wish me luck!' he said.

'Good luck!' said Larry, taking a cigarette.

'Fathers are a curse anyway,' said the other confidentially. 'But I musn't be keeping me little pusher waiting. So long, men.'

'So long,' said Larry and the watchman together.

The policeman disappeared between the high walls of timber, and Larry sat by the brasier and recklessly lit his cigarette. The watchman, too, lit his pipe, and smoked silently and contentedly, spitting now and again out of sheer satisfaction. The faint brightness over the hill showed clearer and clearer, until at last the boy could distinguish the dim outlines of riverside and ships and masts. He shivered. The air seemed to have become colder. The watchman began to mumble complacently to himself within his box.

'Ah, dear me,' he said, launching a spit in the direction of the brasier, 'dear me, honesty is the best policy... Yes, my lady, honesty is the best policy after all, that's what I say... I told you I'd (spit) put a stop to your goings-on, my lady; your (spit) Swedish skippers and your dandy boys, and now you re quiet enough, my lady... Now you're quiet enough.'

Larry rose.

'Where are you going now?' asked the watchman sourly.

'I'm going home,' said Larry.

'Stop where you are now! Didn't you hear what the policeman said?'

'I don't care what the policeman said. I'm going home.'

'Home? Aren't you afraid?'

'What would I be afraid of?' asked Larry contemptuously.

'Ah, my boy,' said the watchman with fierce satisfaction, 'your old fella' will hammer hell out of you when he gets you inside the door!'

'Will he?' asked Larry. 'Will he now? I'd bloody well like to see him try it.' And whistling jauntily, he went off in the direction of the city.

The Duke's Children

Till I was a grown man I could never see precisely what was supposed to be exaggerated in the plots of novelists like Dickens. To this day I can still read about some mysterious street-urchin, brought up to poverty and vice by a rag-picker, who turns out to be the missing heir to an earldom and see nothing peculiar about it. To me it all seems the most natural thing in the world.

Having always been Mother's pet, I was comparatively grown-up when the truth about my own birth broke on me first. In fact I was already at work as a messenger boy on the railway. Naturally, I had played with the idea as I had played with scores of other ideas, but suddenly, almost in a day, every other possibility disappeared, and I knew I had nothing whatever in common with the two commonplace creatures with whom my fate had become so strangely linked.

It wasn't their poverty only that repelled me, though that was bad enough, or the tiny terrace house we lived in with its twelve-foot square of garden in front, its crumbling stumps of gate-posts and low wall that had lost its railing. It was their utter commonness, their squabbles about money, their low friends and fatuous conversations. You could see that no breath of fineness had ever touched them. They seemed like people who had been crippled from birth and never known what it was to walk or run or dance. Though I might be for the moment at least only a messenger, I had those long spells when by some sort of instinct I knew who I really was, could stand aside and watch myself come up the road after my day's work with relaxed and measured steps, turning my head slowly to greet some neighbour and raising my cap with a grace and charm that came of centuries of breeding. Not only could I see myself like that; there were even times when I could hear an interior voice that preceded and dictated each movement as though it were a fragment of a story-book 'He raised his cap gracefully while his face broke into a thoughtful smile.'

And then, as I turned the corner I would see Father at the gate in his house clothes, a ragged trousers and vest, an old cap that came down over his eyes, and boots cut into something that resembled sandals and that he insisted on calling his 'slippers'. Father was a creature of habit. No sooner was he out of his working clothes than he was peppering for his evening paper, and if the newsboy were five minutes late, Father muttered 'I don't know what's coming over that boy at all!' and drifted down to the main road to listen for him. When the newsboy did at last appear, Father would grab the paper from his hand and almost run home, putting on his spectacles awkwardly as he ran and triumphantly surveying the promised treat of the headlines.

And suddenly everything would go black on me, and I would take the chair by the open back door while Father, sitting at the other end, uttered little exclamations of joy or rage and Mother asked anxiously how I had got on during the day. Most of the time I could reply only in monosyllables. How could I tell her that nothing had happened at work that was not as common as the things that happened at home; nothing but those moments of blinding illumination when I was alone in the station yard on a spring morning with sunlight striking the cliffs above the tunnel, and, picking my way between the rails and the trucks, I realised that it was not for long, that I was a duke or earl, lost, stolen or strayed from my proper home and that I had only to be discovered for everything to fall into its place. Illumination came only when I had escaped; most often when I crossed the yard on my way from work and dawdled in the passenger station before the bookstall or watched a passenger train go out on its way to Queenstown or Dublin and realised that one day some train like that would take me back to my true home and patrimony.

These gloomy silences used to make Father mad. He was a talkative man, and every little incident of his day turned into narrative and drama for him. He seemed forever to be meeting old comrades of his army days whom he had not met for fifteen years, and astounding changes had always taken place in them in the meantime. When one of his old friends called, or even when some woman from across the square dropped in for a cup of tea, he would leave everything, even his newspaper, to talk. His corner by the window permitting him no room for drama, he would stamp about the tiny kitchen, pausing at the back door to glance up at the sky or by the other door into the little hallway to see who was passing outside in the Square. It irritated him when I got up in the middle of all this, took my cap and went quietly out. It irritated him even more if I read while he and the others talked, and when some question was addressed to me put down my book and gazed at him blankly. He was so coarse in grain that he regarded it as insolence. He had no experience of dukes, and had never heard that interior voice which dictated my movements and words. 'Slowly the lad lowered the book in which he had been immersed and gazed wonderingly at the man who called himself his father.'

One evening I was coming home from work when a girl spoke to me. Her name was Nancy Harding, and I knew her elder brother slightly. I had never spoken to her indeed, there were not many girls I did speak to. I was too conscious of the fact that though my jacket was good enough, my trousers were an old blue pair of Father's cut down and with a big patch in the seat. But Nancy, emerging from a house near the quarry, hailed me as if we were old friends and walked with me up the road. She was a slim, dark-haired girl with an eager and inconsequent manner, and her chatter bewildered and charmed me. My own conversation was of a rather portentous sort.

'I was down with Madge Regan, getting the answers for my homework,' she explained. 'I don't know what's wrong with me, but I can't do those blooming old sums. Where were you?'

'Oh, I was at work,' I answered.

'At work?' she exclaimed in astonishment. 'Till this hour?'

'I have to work from eight to seven,' I said modestly.

'But, Cripes, aren't they terrible hours?' she said.

'Ah, I'm only filling in time,' I explained lightly. 'I don't expect to be there long'

This was prophetic, because I was sacked a couple of months later, but at the time I just wanted to make it clear that if there was any exploitation being done it was I and not the railway company that was doing it. We walked slowly, and she stood under the gas-lamp at the end of the Square with me. Darkness or day, it was funny how people made a rendezvous of gas-lamps. They were our playrooms when we were kids and our clubs as we became older. And then for the first time I heard the words running through my head as though they were dictating to someone else besides myself. 'Pleased with his quiet conversation and well-bred voice, she wondered if he could really be the son of the Delaneys at all.' Up to this, the voice had paid no attention to other people; now that it had begun to expand its activities it took on a new reality, and I longed to repeat the experience.

I had several opportunities because we met like that a couple of times when I was coming home from work. I was not observant, and it wasn't until years after that it struck me that she might have been waiting for me. And one evening when we were standing under our old gas-lamp I talked a little too enthusiastically about some story-book and Nancy asked for the loan of it. I was pleased with her attention but alarmed at the thought of her seeing where I lived.

'I'll bring it with me tomorrow,' I said.

'Ah, come on and get it for me now,' she said coaxingly, and I glanced over my shoulder and saw Father at the gate, his head cocked listening for the newsboy. I felt suddenly sick. I knew such a nice girl couldn't possibly want to meet Father, but I didn't see how I was to get the book without introducing them. We went up the little uneven avenue together.

'This is Nancy Harding, Dad,' I said in an off-hand tone. 'I just want to get a book for her.'

'Oh, come in, girl, come in,' he said, smiling amiably. 'Sit down, can't you, while you're waiting.' Father's sociability almost caused him to forget the newsboy. 'Min,' he called to Mother, 'you keep an eye on the paper,' and he set a chair in the middle of the kitchen floor. As I searched in the front room for the book, which in my desperation I could not find, I heard Mother go for the paper and Father talking away like mad to Nancy, and when I went into the kitchen, there he was in his favourite chair, the paper lying unopened on the table beside him while he told an endless, pointless story about old times in the neighbourhood. Father had been born in the neighbourhood which he seemed to think a matter for pride, but if there was one of Father's favourite subjects I could not stand it was the still wilder and more sordid life people had lived there when he was growing up. This story was about a wake all his juiciest stories were about wakes and a tired woman getting jealous of the corpse in the bed. He was so pleased with Nancy's attention that he was dramatising even more than usual, and I stood silent in the kitchen door for several minutes with a ducal air of scorn before he even noticed me. As I saw Nancy to the road I felt humiliated to the depths of my being. I noticed that the hallway was streaming with damp, that our gate was only a pair of brick stumps from which the cement had fallen away and that the Square, which had never been adopted by the Council, was full of washing. There were two washerwomen on the terrace, each with a line of her own.

But that wasn't the worst. One evening when I came home Mother said joyously:

'Oh, your dad ran into that nice little Harding girl on his way home.'

'Oh, did he?' I asked indifferently though feeling I had been kicked hard in the stomach.

'Oh, my goodness!' Father exclaimed, letting down his paper for a moment and crowing. 'The way that one talks! Spatter! spatter! spatter! And, by the way,' he added, looking at me over his glasses, 'her aunt Lil used to be a great friend of your mother's at one time. Her mother was a Clancy. I knew there was something familiar about her face.'

'I'd never have recognised it,' Mother said gravely. 'Such a quiet little woman as Miss Clancy used to be.'

'Oh, begor there's nothing quiet about that piece,' chortled Father but he did not sound disapproving. Father liked young people with something to say for themselves not like me.

I was mortified. It was bad enough not seeing Nancy myself, but to have her meet Father like that in his working clothes coming from the manure factory down the Glen, and hear him as I had no doubt she did hear him talk in his ignorant way about me was too much. I could not help contrasting Father with Mr Harding whom I occasionally met coming from work and whom I looked at with a respect that bordered on reverence. He was a small man with a face like a clenched fist, always very neatly dressed, and he usually carried his newspaper rolled up like a baton and sometimes hit his thigh with it as he strode briskly home.

One evening when I glanced shyly at him he nodded in his brusque way. Everything about him was brusque, keen, and soldierly, and when I saw that he recognised me I swung into step beside him. He was like a military procession with a brass band, the way he always set the pace for anyone who accompanied him. 'Where are you working now?' he asked sharply with a sideglance at me. 'Oh, on the railway still,' I said. 'Just for a few months anyway.'

'And what are you doing there?'

'Oh, just helping in the office,' I replied lightly. I knew this was not exactly true but I hated to tell anybody that I was only a messenger boy.

'Of course I study in my spare time,' I added hastily. It was remarkable how the speeding up of my pace seemed to speed up my romancing as well. There was something breathless about the man that left me breathless too. 'I thought of taking the Indian Civil Service exam or something of the sort. There's no future in railways.'

'Isn't there?' he asked with some surprise.

'Not really,' I answered indifferently. 'Another few years and it will all be trucks. I really do it only as a stop-gap. I wouldn't like to take any permanent job unless I could travel. Outside Ireland

I mean. You see, languages are my major interest.' 'Are they?' he asked in the same tone. 'How many do you know?'

'Oh, only French and German at the moment I mean enough to get round with,' I said. The pace was telling on me. I felt I wasn't making the right impression. Maybe to be a proper linguist you needed to know a dozen languages. I mended my hand as best I could. 'I'm going to do Italian and Spanish this winter if I get time. You can't get anywhere in the modern world without Spanish. After English it's the most spoken of them all.' 'Go on!' he said.

I wasn't altogether pleased with the result of this conversation. The moment I had left him I slowed down to a gentle stroll, and this made me realise that the quick march had committed me further than I liked to go. All I really knew of foreign languages was a few odd words and phrases, like echoes of some dream of my lost fatherland, which I learned and repeated to myself with a strange vague pleasure. It was not prudent to pretend that I knew the languages thoroughly. After all, Mr Harding had three daughters, all well-educated. People were always being asked to his house, and I had even been encouraging myself with the prospect of being asked as well. But now, if I were invited it would mainly be because of my supposed knowledge of foreign languages, and when Nancy or one of her sisters burst into fluent French or German my few poetic phrases would not be much help. I needed something more practical, something to do with railways, for preference. I had an old French phrase-book which I had borrowed from somebody, and I determined to learn as much as I could of this by heart.

I worked hard, spurred on by an unexpected meeting with Nancy's eldest sister, Rita, who suddenly stopped and spoke to me on the road though to my astonishment and relief she spoke in English.

Then, one evening when I was on my usual walk, which in those days nearly always brought me somewhere near Nancy's house, I ran into her going in, and we stood at the street corner near her home. I was pleased with this because Rita came out soon afterwards and said in a conspiratorial tone 'Why don't ye grab the sofa before Kitty gets it?' which made Nancy blush, and then her father passed and nodded to us. I waved back to him, but Nancy had turned her back as he appeared so that she did not see him. I drew her attention to him striding down the road, but somehow this only put her in mind of my father.

'I saw him again the other day,' she said with a smile that hurt me.

'Did you?' I asked with a sniff. 'What was he talking about? His soldiering days?'

'No,' she said with interest. 'Does he talk about them?'

'Does he ever talk about anything else?' I replied wearily. 'I have that last war off by heart. It seems to have been the only thing that ever happened to him.'

'He knows a terrible lot, though, doesn't he?' she asked.

'He's managed to conceal it pretty well,' I replied. 'The man is an out-and-out failure, and he's managed to turn Mother into one as well. I suppose she had whatever brains there were between them which wasn't much, I'm afraid.'

'Go on!' said Nancy with a bewildered air. 'Then why did she marry him?'

'"Echo answers why,"' I said with a laugh at being able to get in a phrase that had delighted me in some story-book. 'Oh, I suppose it was the usual thing.' And when I saw her gaping at me in wonderment I shrugged my shoulders and added contemptuously, 'Lust.'

Nancy blushed again and made to leave.

'Well, it's well to be you,' she said, 'knowing what's wrong with him. God alone knows what's wrong with mine.'

I was sorry she had to go in such a hurry but pleased with the impression of culture and sophistication I had managed to convey, and I looked forward to showing off a bit more when I went to one of their Sunday evening parties. With that, and some really practical French, I could probably get anywhere. At the same time it struck me that they were very slow about asking me, and my evening walked past their house took on a sort of stubborn defiance. At least, I wouldn't let them ignore me. It wasn't until weeks later that the bitter truth dawned on me that I was not being invited because nobody wanted me there. Nancy had seen my home and talked to my parents; her sisters and father had seen me, and all of them had seen my cut-down trousers with the patch on the seat. It mattered nothing to them even if I spoke French and German like an angel, even if I were liable to be sent off to India in the next few months. They did not think I was their class.

Those were the bitterest weeks of my life. With a sort of despair I took my evening walk in the early winter days past their house but never saw anybody, and as I turned up the muddy lane behind it and heard the wind moaning in the   branches, and looked down across the sloping field to their house, nestling in the hollow with the light shining brilliantly in the kitchen where the girls did their homework, it seemed to be full of all the beauty I would never know. Sometimes, leaning over the lane wall and watching it, it even seemed possible that I was what they thought, not the son of a Duke but the son of a labourer in the manure factory; but at other times, walking home by myself, tired and dispirited, the truth blazed up angrily in me again, and I knew that when it became known, the Hardings would be the first to regret their blindness. At such times I was always making brilliant loveless matches and then revealing coldly to Nancy that I had never cared for anyone but herself.

It was at the lowest depth of my misery that I was introduced to a girl called May Dwyer, and somehow, from the first moment, I found that there was no need for me to indulge in invention. Invention and May would never have gone together. She had a directness of approach I had never met with before in a girl. The very first evening I saw her home she asked me if I could afford the tram fare. That shocked me but afterwards I was grateful. Then she asked me in to see her parents which scared me stiff, but I promised to come in another night when it wasn't so late, and at once she told me which evenings she was free. It was not forwardness or lightness in her; it was all part of a directness that made her immediately both a companion and a sweetheart. I owe her a lot, for without her I might still be airing my French and German to any woman who attracted me.

Even when I did go in with her for a cup of tea I felt at home after the first few minutes. Of course, May asked me if I wanted to go upstairs, a thing no woman had ever suggested before to me, and I blushed, but by this time I was becoming used to her methods. Her father was a long, sad Civil Servant, and her mother a bright, direct little woman not unlike May herself, and whatever he said, the pair of them argued with and jeered him unmercifully. This only made him hang his head lower, but suddenly, after I had been talking for a while he began to argue with me about the state of the country, which seemed to cause him a lot of concern. In those days I was very optimistic on the subject, and I put my hands deep in my trousers pockets and answered him back politely but warmly. Then he caught me out on a matter of fact, and suddenly he gave a great crow of delight and went out to bring in two bottles of Guinness. By this time I was so much in my element that I accepted the Guinness; I always have loved a good argument.

'Cripes!' May said when I was leaving, 'do you ever stop once you start?'

'It's not so often I meet an intelligent talker,' I said loftily.

'When you've heard as much of my old fellow as I have, maybe you won't think he's so intelligent,' she said, but she did not sound indignant, and I had an impression that she was really quite pleased at having brought home a young fellow who could entertain her father. It gave her the feeling that she was really all the time an intellectual but had met the wrong sort of boy. In the years I was courting her we quarrelled like hell, but between her father and me it was a case of love at first sight. After I was fired from the railway, it was he who got me another job and insisted on my looking after it. The poor devil had always been pining for a man in the house.

Then one evening I ran into Nancy Harding whom I had not seen for some months. It was an embarrassing moment because I realised at once that my fantasy had all come true. If I had not

actually made a brilliant match, I had as good as I done so, and
yet she was my first and purest love.

'I hear you and May Dwyer are very great these days,' she said and
something in her tone struck me as peculiar. Afterwards I realised
that it was the tone I was supposed to adopt when I broke the
news to her.

'I've seen quite a lot of her,' I admitted.

'You weren't long getting hooked,' she went on with a smile that
somehow did not come off

'I don't know about being "hooked" as you call it,' I said, getting
on my dignity at once. 'She asked me to her house and I went,
that's all.'

'Oh, we know all about it,' said Nancy, and this time there was
no mistaking the malice in her tone. 'You don't have to tell me
anything.'

'Well, there isn't so much to tell,' I replied with a bland smile.

'And I suppose she talks French and German like a native?' asked
Nancy.   This reference to the falsehoods I had told did hurt me.
I had known they were indiscreet, but it hadn't occurred to me
that they would become a joke in the Harding family.

'I don't honestly know what you're talking about, Nancy,' I said
weakly. 'May asked me to her house and I went, just as I'd have
gone to yours if you'd asked me. That's all there is to it.'

'Oh, is that all?' she asked in her commonest tone, and suddenly
to my astonishment I saw tears in her eyes. 'And if you had a
house like mine you wouldn't mind asking people there either,
would you? And sisters like mine! And a father like mine! It's all
very well for you to grouse about your old fellow, but if you had
one like mine you'd have something to talk about. Blooming old
pig, wouldn't open his mouth to you. 'Tis easy for you to talk,
Larry Delaney! Damn easy!'

And then she shot away from me to conceal her tears, and I was
left standing there on the pavement, stunned. Too stunned really
to have done anything about it. It had all happened too suddenly,
and been too great an intrusion on my fantasy for me to grasp it
at all. I was so astonished and upset that though I was to have met

May that night I didn't go. Instead I went for a lonely walk by myself over the hills to the river to think what I should do about it. In the end, of course, I did nothing at all; I had no experience to indicate to me what I could do; and it was not until years later that I even realised that the reason I had cared so much for Nancy was that she, like myself, was one of the Duke's children, one of those outcasts of a lost fatherland who go through life, living above and beyond themselves like some image of man's original aspiration.

Private Property

My mother was never really happy about my being in the secret revolutionary army, and Father hated it. Father was a natural conservative who hated change on principle, and he had a shrewd idea of the sort of family whose lack of balance would cause them to be mixed up in it. Having relatives in the lunatic asylum would naturally be a predisposing factor. Another would be having come from some backward place like Carlow. Father disliked my great friend, Mick Ryan, for no other reason than that.

Now, I was a well-balanced young fellow. I will say that for myself. I didn't drink; I smoked very little; I was regular at work and contributed my fair share to the housekeeping. So I didn't fly off the handle as another might have done, and I did my best to explain to Father that this was all only passion and prejudice on his part, that nothing would ever improve if it depended on people like him, and that it didn't really matter who a man was or where he came from. It had no effect on Father. He didn't want things improved. He wanted them to last out his lifetime the way they were.

He tried to keep me in check by making me be home at ten, but I felt that as a revolutionist as well as a wage earner, I had to stick out for half past. It was the old story. He wouldn't give me a key and go to bed like a sensible man. One lock wasn't enough for him. The world was too uncertain with thieves and murderers forever on the prowl. He had three separate bolts on the front door and had to bolt them himself before he could sleep. There was no use arguing with a man like that.

We of the secret army met in a Gaelic League hall in a back street and discussed dispatches from Dublin telling us to be armed and ready for the great day. I didn't see how we were to arm ourselves at all, the way things were going. Our Quartermaster a stocky little stone-mason called Johnny Forrestal was a bitter old pill who had been a revolutionary from the age of fifteen and had been in five gaols and on three hunger strikes. He was above suspicion, and almost above criticism by kids like ourselves, but he had no luck. As soon as ever we scraped together a few pounds from the men's subscriptions and bought a couple of rifles the police nosed them out. It was making us all depressed, and the Adjutant, Tom Harrison, was really savage. He said Johnny was too old, but I knew it wasn't Johnny's age that came against him; it was his vanity.

Johnny simply couldn't walk down a street in that stocky portentous way of his without advertising that he was a man who had fought in two wars and was only waiting his chance to fight in a third. He had toadies who gave him all the admiration he needed, and I suspected that he spilled everything to them.

But if Johnny was tough, Harrison was tougher. He was a grocer's curate from down the country and looked like a seminarist in mufti. He was a man who never hesitated to speak his mind, and as this was a privilege Johnny liked to reserve for himself, there was always bad blood between them.

'I tell you again there's a spy in the camp,' Harrison shouted one night we were discussing the latest catastrophe.

'Maybe you'd tell us who he is,' Johnny said with a face on him like one of his own tombstones.

'If I knew he wouldn't be there long,' said Harrison.

'You'd shoot him, I suppose?' Johnny asked with a sneer.

'I would shoot him.'

'He got no information out of me anyway,' Johnny said in a surly tone. 'I could keep my mouth shut before some people here were born.'

This was Johnny at his old game of turning the discussion into a vote of confidence, and he'd done it too often for my liking.

'I'm afraid I agree with Tom, Johnny,' I said.

'Then why don't you do the job yourself?' asked Johnny, leaving it to be understood what would happen if I did.

'I don't want to make a personal matter of it, Johnny,' I said, keeping my temper.

'And I *do* want to make a personal matter of it,' said Harrison, losing his. 'Damn it, we're only wasting our own time till we learn to keep our equipment safe. I say Larry is the man for the job.'

So that was how, at the age of seventeen, I came to be Brigade Quartermaster, and, though it may sound like self-praise, they never had a better. Mick Ryan was a tower of strength to me. He was a tall, handsome, reckless devil who worked on the railway, and the pair of us made a grand team because he made me do things that ordinarily I'd have been too shy to do, while I stopped him doing things he would have done when his imagination ran away with him. In the evenings we went into pubs on the quays, talking to sailors and giving assumed names. When we began, we had only one Smith and Wesson pistol belonging to Mick's brother who was in the British Army, and even for this we had only Thompson gun ammunition, but within six months we were getting in guns from Hamburg and Lisbon and packing them away in a dump we had built on the hill behind the church. Mick and I had dug it out ourselves and propped it with railway sleepers. We even put an old bed in it so that we could sleep there. Not that I ever stayed out all night, but Mick was a bit of a rambler.

By this time the police were beginning to realise that it wasn't old Johnny Forrestal they had to deal with and they panicked. Dwyer, the superintendent, called the detectives together and warned them that there would be sackings if something wasn't done. They did their best but it wasn't very good. You could see that someone had tipped them off about me and Mick because our houses were watched by detectives with bikes, and we made a new game out of giving them the slip.

To tell the truth, I was a bit flattered by all this attention. It was the first time that anyone had taken me seriously. At first, Father couldn't believe it, and after that he was stunned. He stood for hours behind the curtains in the front room, watching the detectives, and sometimes getting mad with the detective and sometimes with me. He discovered that the detective's wife kept hens, so he dropped poisoned bread in her garden. At the same time he tried to make me stay in at night, but no Brigade Quartermaster with an ounce of self-respect could let himself be locked in at ten. Father locked me out, but behind his back Mother left the window open. Then he fastened the window catch himself but I got over the back wall. After that he contented himself with muttering prophecies to himself about what was in store for me.

'Aha, they think they're cleverer than their fathers, but they'll be taught. Mark my words! The rope will teach them. Then they'll see how clever they were.'

I made a point of it that no one should know the whereabouts of the dump except Mick, myself and Harrison. Mick was opposed even to Harrison's knowing, but, seeing that both of us were liable to be picked up any day, I thought this was carrying secrecy too far.

Besides, I knew that Mick was prejudiced against Harrison for reasons that had nothing to do with the organisation. In his own way Mick was as bad as Father. It was one of the main drawbacks of the movement private quarrels and I was forever begging Mick to keep out of them and think only of the principle. But Mick hadn't a principle in his head; he liked or hated people, and that was all there was to it.

Now the reason he hated Harrison was this. Harrison was married to the sister of Mick's friend, Joe Ward, another member of the organisation and as decent a poor devil as ever drew breath, only for his misfortune. He had married a flighty woman who bore him four kids but omitted to make a proper home for them because the horses took up all her spare time and money. Between illness and debt poor Joe was half-distracted. Mick, being a single man and very open-handed, was always helping him, but Harrison at least according to Mick would do nothing for him. This cut poor Joe to the heart because he was an emotional man, always laughing or crying; he dearly loved his sister, and, when she married Harrison, he had given them a magnificent clock as a wedding present something he could badly afford.

Now, I didn't doubt that for a moment, but I could see Harrison's point of view as well. That was always my trouble; being a reasonable man I could see everyone's point of view. After all, Harrison was a married man, too, with a kid of his own, and he wasn't earning so much in the grocery and bar that he could afford to be generous on Mick's scale. Besides, I had the feeling that helping Joe was really an acute case of casting your bread upon the waters. Personally, I would have been damn full sure it wouldn't come back.

But for the sake of the organisation I tried to keep the peace between Mick and Harrison. I praised them both to one another, and any little admission I could wring out of one I passed on to the other. It was all for the cause. I was a conscientious officer, even if I was only seventeen, and in those days I was innocent enough to believe that this was all that was needed to keep Ireland united.

That was where the ferry-boat left me. It began innocently enough the day Joe Ward discovered that his wife had been to a money-lender and borrowed seven pounds. To poor Joe, weighed down with troubles, this seemed like the end of the world. He was never what you'd call a well-balanced man, and for a while he was probably a bit off his head. Instead of going to his sister, who might have raised a few shillings for him unknown to Harrison, or to Mick, who would have borrowed the money himself to help him, he went to the pub where Harrison worked. He stood at the door with his hands out and the tears streaming down his long clown's face and said dramatically: 'Look at me, Tom Harrison! Look at me! Happier men floated out Lough Mahon.'

Now, in spite of what happened afterwards, I want to be quite fair about this. Though Mick called Harrison a mean bastard, my own impression of him was that he wasn't a bad chap at all, really, and that, given time to get used to the idea, he might have done something substantial for Joe. I understood his position. I might have taken the cautious line myself, for after all, where was this thing going to end?

'Begor, Joe,' he said, 'if I had it you'd be welcome, but the way it is with me, I haven't.'

'I'm sorry for your troubles, poor man,' said Joe with withering scorn and stalked out on him. Of course, Harrison was leaping. After all, be had only been playing for time, and while it's bad enough to be asked for money, it's a hard thing to be insulted when you don't fall over yourself giving it. I sympathised with Harrison. As I say, the only excuse I could see for Joe was that he wasn't in his right mind at the time. I saw his point of view, too, of course. That's the worst of being a fair-minded man; you can't buy any friends with half-hearted sympathy.

Well, next evening, when I was pushing my bicycle back up Summerhill from work, who did I see but Harrison, coming towards me, looking very serious. He barely saluted me.

'Nothing wrong, is there, Tom?' I asked.

'Plenty, I'm afraid,' he said stiffly, and made to go on.

'Nothing to do with the organisation, Tom?' I asked, turning the bike and walking back down the hill with him. Of course, it was the organisation that was on my mind.

'Oh, nothing,' he said in the same tone. 'A purely private matter.' You could take it to mean I should mind my own business, but I didn't think he intended it that way. I could see he was very upset. 'Larceny!' he said then. 'Burglary! My house broken into and looted while I was at work. Oh, nothing to do with the organisation!'

'For God's sake!' I said. 'Was much taken?'

'Oh, only a clock!' he snapped, and then, in case I might think he hadn't enough cause to be in a state about it: 'A valuable clock.' The word struck a familiar chord, but for a while I couldn't place it. Then I remembered where I'd heard of that clock before.

'That wouldn't be the clock Joe Ward gave you, Tom?' I asked.

'It would,' he said, stopping to give me a suspicious glance. 'It is. How do you know about it?'

'Oh, only that Mick Ryan mentioned it to me once,' I said in confusion.

'Whoever gave it, the clock is my property now,' said Harrison, moving on.

'And what are you going to do about it?' I asked.

'I'm going to put the police on him,' Harrison said defiantly, and I knew by his truculent tone that he was a bit ashamed of himself. To us, of course, the police were never anything but enemy spies. It gave me a nasty turn. Besides, I was tired and beginning to feel that to keep our fellows together would take more than compliments.

'On who, Tom?' I asked.

'Who do you think? On Ward, of course. It's about time that fellow was taught a lesson.'

I had not been thinking of anyone in particular, and the name gave me a start. Then I could feel myself getting red with embarrassment.

'Oh, was it Joe took it?' I said.

'Walked into the house and took it from under my wife's eyes,' Harrison said indignantly.

'And you're going to put the enemy police on him?' I asked.

'Who else is there, man?' he retorted hotly.

'Well, I was thinking that maybe the organisation might do something,' I said.

'And while I was waiting for the organisation to do it my clock would be sold.'

'Oh, I'm not criticising you,' I said. 'I was only thinking of the effect it would have on young fellows in the organisation an officer going to the enemy about another member.'

'But damn it, man, if someone broke into your house tonight and stole valuable property wouldn't you do the same?' he asked.

'If I had any property, and the man was a common thief, I dare say I would,' I admitted.

'There's nothing uncommon about Joe Ward only his impudence,' said Harrison. 'Now it's all very well to talk, Larry,' he went on in a more reasonable tone, 'and you and I agree about most things, but whatever government you have, you must protect private property. Even an army of occupation has to do that.'

'Oh, I'm not denying it, Tom,' I said, making the best I could of an argument that was a bit abstract for me. 'Only I don't think you're being fair to poor Joe. I don't really, Tom. My own impression is that the man can't have been right in the head.'

'He was sufficiently right in his head to come to my house while I was out at work,' said Harrison.

So we went on together, past the church at the foot of the hill and over the New Bridge, with me still arguing for the sake of appearances. It was the organisation I was thinking of, and the scandal and disagreements that were bound to follow, with some of the lads backing Harrison and others backing Joe Ward, but nothing was farther from Harrison's mind. He hadn't a principle in his head any more than Father or Mick. All he could think of was his blooming old clock. I knew if he didn't do something about it he wouldn't sleep, only lie awake, noticing the silence in the house, and mourning for his clock as if it was someone that had died on him. I felt gloomy and desperate. It was a spring evening, coming on to dusk, and the metal bridges and the back streets full of old warehouses gave me the creeps. There seemed to be no hope for idealism, the way things were.

I remained outside on the quay while Harrison went into the barracks. It was a big, red-brick building with a few lights burning. I wondered if I should be there at all and what I'd say about it to the lads at our next meeting. I decided that there was nothing wrong in waiting since the man was so upset. It was the same thing as with Mick. He'd get in a bake, and do something he shouldn't, and then regret it after. It all came of a want of principle.

Nothing happened for a long time, and I began to wonder whether Dwyer, the superintendent, hadn't taken the chance of locking Harrison up. There was a light in his office, which I recognised because I had plans of the whole building in the dump. I saw a figure come to the window and look up and down the river and decided that I'd better get a move on quick. I jumped on the bicycle and started to ride away. Then I glanced back and saw two detectives get into a car and follow me. I got cold all over because I knew I had no way of escape. But then the car passed me out and I realised that they had not been following me at all. I decided to follow them instead. I had a good notion of where they were going, and I knew Harrison would be inside till they came back.

They stopped outside a tenement house on another quay. There were no curtains in the windows and no lights but candles. A couple of women were leaning out of the windows and they began to pretend the police had come to call on them. The detectives paid no attention and walked straight in the hallway as though they knew where they were going.

When they came out three minutes later, each of them was carrying a clock. Joe Ward followed them out in his shirt sleeves, a thin, consumptive man with glasses and a mad air. He stood on the steps of the house and addressed the detectives and the crowd that had gathered. Like all emotional men, he laughed as if he was crying, and cried as if he was laughing, and only that I knew him so well I'd have laughed at him myself.

'There's the great Irish patriot for you!' he bawled, waving one arm wildly. 'There's the great Republican chief, General Tom Harrison, putting the Free State police on his own poor misfortunate brother-in-law, and all over an old clock! A clock I gave him for his wedding when 'tis a dose of poison I should have given him! There's the great patriot, a fellow that wouldn't lend you a bob if the children died of hunger at his feet. God help Ireland and God help the poor! Give me back my own clock anyway, ye robbers of hell! Give me back the clock I bought with my own couple of ha'pence!'

They ignored him and drove off. This time they got well away from me and I only arrived back at the barracks in time to see Harrison coming out. He had his own clock under his arm, wrapped up, and you could see the comfort it gave him. He wasn't the same man at all. That is the only way I can describe him. He was bubbling with good nature towards myself and the whole world, and nothing would do him only to unwrap the clock for me to admire it. It was a good clock all right.

'Ah, it may teach that fellow some sense,' he said, but there wasn't a hint of indignation left in him, nothing but his own basic good humour. 'He should know better than to think he can get away with things like that.'

With the picture of Joe fresh in my mind, I didn't feel like discussing it. I had the impression that poor Joe would get away with damn little in this world or the next. In a curious way I began to understand Mick Ryan's attitude to Harrison. It was against my principles but I couldn't help it.

'Who did you see inside?' I asked.

'You'd never believe,' said Harrison with a chuckle.

'Not Dwyer, surely?' I asked. I could hardly believe that Dwyer would concern himself about a thing like a stolen clock.

'Oh, one of the detectives recognised me, of course,' said Harrison. 'Dwyer came down himself and brought me up to his office to wait. He took it more seriously than I did, as a matter of fact, but I suppose he has to; it's his job. He told them to bring in every clock in the place. They brought two.'

'I saw them at it,' I said.

'Did you follow them?' he asked eagerly. 'What happened?'

'Joe came out and made a bit of a scene. There was a crowd.'

'Tell me, Larry, was he mad?'

It was all too palsy-walsy for me.

'He was upset. You'd hardly blame him.'

'I do not blame him, Larry,' Harrison said gravely. 'I'm genuinely sorry for that unfortunate wretch. We all told him what that woman was like, but he wouldn't believe us. God knows, if there was anything I could do for him, I'd do it.'

The benevolence that clock produced in Harrison was simply astonishing. He was so full of good nature that he never even noticed that I didn't share it with him.

'Tell us about Dwyer,' I said to get away from it.

'Oh, he stood me a drink, man,' said Harrison, beginning to chuckle again. 'You should have come in with me. You'd have enjoyed it.'

'I saw him in the window.'

'Oh, he saw you as well. There are no flies on Dwyer.'

'Did he ask any questions?'

'Questions? He never stopped.'

'About what?'

'About you and Ryan and the dump. Oh, naturally pretending to have a great admiration for us all, particularly you. He said he was like that himself when he was younger. Like hell he was … Stand in here for a minute.' He whispered the last words, glancing hastily over his shoulder to see if we were being followed, and then pulled me into a dark archway. He was very excited.

'Do you know that he offered me money to tell him where the dump was?' he whispered angrily. 'Big money! He said the organisation was riddled with spies; that every gun Johnny Forrestal bought was reported to him twice over inside twenty-four hours. They meet him after midnight at some hideout of his in town.'

I believed him, unfortunately, and my feeling of gloom deepened. Of course, I had always suspected that there was a spy, but it was a different thing to be sure of it. For the future I knew that I should trust nobody. All the same I wasn't feeling so kindly towards Harrison as to look for sympathy from him.

'I was afraid of that,' I said. 'I guessed Johnny talked too much. Dwyer isn't getting the information now though.'

'That's what I told him,' said Harrison. 'He said he was getting plenty, but that's only bluff. Otherwise, why would he offer to bribe me? … But imagine it! Fellows you'd be drinking with one minute stealing down there the next to swear your life away. What sort of conscience can they-have?'

'If they have a conscience,' I said despondently. In the badly lit street, supperless, cold and tired, I was beginning to wonder if there was any opportunity for idealism, and if Father wasn't right after all.

'Dwyer laughed at me when I said that,' said Harrison ruefully as he walked on. "'Nonsense, man,' he said. 'I could put a call through on that telephone this minute and bring in two men you know well that are giving information about you, and you'd damn soon see they're not so different from yourself. Poor devils! Maybe they got into a spot of trouble over a woman and they wanted the money.'"

'They couldn't do without women, I suppose,' I said. Naturally, at seventeen they were about the last thing I wanted.

And then, three weeks later, the dump was raided and everything in it seized, including Mick Ryan with all the Brigade papers on him. It was a pure fluke that I wasn't there myself. Mick, who was a resourceful chap, got rid of the papers by distributing cigarettes wholesale to the detectives and lighting them with letters he pulled from his pockets. Only for that, I'd have been in gaol with him. From the barracks he slipped me out a note that just read: 'Shoot Harrison'. Mick was a dramatic sort of fellow on occasions.

Of course, I didn't shoot Harrison. To begin with, I hadn't any absolute proof, though I didn't need it. I was sick at the loss of my priceless dump, all the lovely rifles and automatics smuggled in from all over Europe, and all sold over an old clock. If I were to have Harrison shot it would mean that I would have to start again from the beginning, and I didn't have the heart. I just dropped out of the organisation altogether.

Father was very cocked-up about Mick's arrest because it confirmed his old prejudice against Carlow people, and the first night the detective failed to show up near the house he positively purred. He gave me five shillings for myself and told me that in future I could stay out until eleven. 'Or so,' he added. He didn't want to seem severe, and he had been a bit wild himself at my age. It was the first time he had been civil to me for a year and a half, and I got so sentimental that I broke down and told him the whole story. To my astonishment he flew into a wild rage and wanted to know why I didn't chuck a bomb into Harrison's house. That very night he took a pot of white paint and a brush and painted the front wall of Harrison's house with the words 'Spies and Informers Beware'. God, you can never tell with Conservatives!

I took the five bob, but I was home by half past ten. I had decided to go to the School of Commerce in the evenings. I was beginning to see that there was no future in revolutions — not in Ireland, anyway. It may be different elsewhere.

Alec

When I came home from the column Henderson, the Quarter-master, told me glumly that the only fighting man we had left in our company area was Alec Gorman. The company, that splen-did company that had been trained to form fours, turn, wheel, and march like regular soldiers, the company was gone, and in its place a solitary Cuchulain at the ford, stood Alec. Now, Alec had never belonged to us, he was too much of an idler. Idler, lounger at bars, tippler, scrounge, football fan, pry, gossip, and maker of quarrels: that was Alec.

Every town has its own Irishtown and every Irishtown its Alec. He was known to everybody. He was welcome at every pub for miles around. Even the old women came to him to take sides in their fights. For instance, when he passed Kate Nagle's door that old rogue would look out, or mount the three-legged stool she used to look over the lane wall with, and shout after him.

'Alec Gorman, how high up in the world we're getting! You passed me by yesterday without as much as 'Good morrow'!'

'Is it a man you want, Kate?' Alec would shout back.

'Ah, you blackguard!' the old woman would bawl delightedly. 'I'd get a better one than you in the Salvation Army or the Incurable Hospital.'

'You ugly old hake, and you're eighty if you're a day! How well you wouldn't ask if I'd a mouth on me.'

'Come in and search me, Alec boy.'

'Will you give us a look at the old stocking?'

'Come in, come in, putty-nose!' And to crown it all Alec would go in and talk to her by the hour.

One night I was sent for by Alec to go to Miss Mac's public-house. We stood by the bar sipping pints of porter. He had dropped his voice to a whisper, and the crowd drew back as it were to leave us more alone. Alec was very tall, a splendidly-built boy with a long bright face, a nose that was a little flattened by nature (which caused Kate Nagle to speak of him as she did), and great, blue, wandering eyes. He wore an old navy coat and riding-breeches, leaned a little over his drink and me, and with one hand fondling the glass held on with the other to a revolver in his breeches pocket. Now and again he called a halt to fling a joke at the red-haired barmaid or raise a squabble with one of the men at the bar.

People came in and went out, old women with pint pots under their tartan shawls or little children with quart bottles wrapped in brown paper, and Alec spoke so low it was impossible to guess what he wanted. It seemed to have something to do with rifles that had to be shifted to a place of safety, but sometimes he called the rifles shovels, and sometimes butter-boxes (not to mention traps, yokes and gadgets), and talked about a letter from the shop (which I took to mean Brigade Headquarters), and about the butter-boxes being in cold storage. He was also expecting Peter Keary, and he spoke Peter's name literally without a movement of his lips, watching all the time from under his eyes to see if anyone was listening.

It appeared, too, that during the evening he had found himself in fresh trouble. By his account Kate Nagle was standing quietly upon her three-legged stool to get a view into the roadway — at peace with the world as he said when a quarrel blew up between herself and Najax opposite. Najax was a woman who leaned over her half-door a good deal; a pale, untidy, reckless, handsome woman with a wastrel of a husband and the temper of a fiend. Old Kate had been putting it about in her malicious way that Najax was a Free State spy, and within five minutes the argument between them had drawn half Irishtown to its doors.

'We're short of men and we're short of guns,' said old Kate, 'but there's bullets enough behind us yet!'

What did that mean?, Najax asked the neighbours. What did it mean? Who were the bullets for? What were the bullets for?

'To give you and your misbegotten likes the hunt,' said Kate in a solemn and reverent tone, launching a spit that reached to the middle of the road.

'Who'll give me the hunt, you old serpent?' screamed Najax.

'Ireland has friends yet, Norah Gillespie!'

'May the devil chase the friends of Ireland!' bawled Najax. 'May the devil chase the friends of Ireland — and your friends too, Antichrist!' bawled Najax. 'You never had friends but for what they could get out of you.'

Those were the words of Najax as reported to Alex by Kate Nagle. Innocent enough, you will agree, but Alec in his simple way went off into a rage. Who was the friend that stuck to Kate for what could be got out of her? Himself, of course, that was clear. Besides, it had been publicly wished that the devil might chase the friends of Ireland. What friend of Ireland was clearly indicated? Himself again. It was treason to the Republic and a libel on him. So Alec crossed the road to Najax's house, and stamped in on top of her, blustering and swearing. Najax retorted by giving him sauce. Then he lifted up a bath of sudsy water that was on the table before her and threw it at her head, leaving her with her own nightdress hung about her neck, dripping with water. The rest of the clothes that she had been washing he kicked all round the floor in a perfect fury.

This was Alec when he was quite himself.

Most of the men in the bar were British ex-soldiers. Since Alec was a child he had been listening to the stories they had to tell, stories about the war in Africa and India and the big war in France. Now Alec had pushed them aside to make stories for himself, and they accepted the position without malice. I was listening to one of them crooning in a corner a song about the great war:

The troopship now is sailing, and my poor heart is breaking.
The troopship now is sailing, all bound for Germany . . .

when another came up to me and held out his hand.

'I knew your father, Larry,' he said.

'Did you now?' said I, not knowing what else to say, and shaking hands with him.

'I did then.'

'Go on now, Mike,' said Alec. 'Unless you're going to stand a drink.'

'I knew his father,' said Mike, turning upon Alec. 'A good soldier of her late Majesty, God rest her! I knew the father and I know the son. I won't breathe a word, not wan word.' He turned away from us.

'Aren't you going to stand that drink you bloody *oinseach*?' said Alec with a screech.

Mike turned round on us again and lifted his right hand high in the air — a royal gesture. He wasn't going to stand a drink, but he came back solemnly step by step while everybody in the bar looked on and listened.

'When I was in South Africa —' he said.

'Ah, shut up about South Africa!' said Alec. 'What about the drink?'

'When I was in Pretoria, I went into a bar one day. There was three of us there. A bar, just like this. There is a young man behind the counter. "This and that," says Mackerel, one of the men that was with me, calling for the drinks, "this and that." The drinks are filled out. "Where are you from?" says Mackerel, looking closely at the young man. "London," he says. "Did you ever see this before?" says Mackerel, pointing to the badge in his own cap, it was the Munsters' badge. "Maybe I did," says the other. "Maybe you did too," says Mackerel coolly. "Where's that you said you were from?" "London." "Say this after me," says Mackerel

"I have wandered an exile 'mid cold-hearted strangers,
Far, far from my home and the beautiful Lee."

"Go on now," says the man. "Say it," says Mackerel sweetly. "I will not say it," says the other. "Say it, I tell you," says Mackerel, cooing like a dove. "No," says the other, "I won't." "Do you know what you are?" says Mackerel in a flash, jumping the counter like a three-year-old, "you're an informer from Ireland," and, says he, whipping off his belt, "so help me, Christ, you'll never leave this bar alive." '

Just as he finished the story Peter Keary strolled in. He saluted everyone at the bar. The old soldier touched his cap and stood back.

'Evening, sir.' He turned to me again and went on in a whisper, 'That's true, d'ye understand? True, every word of it!' Then he stood to attention and rapped out an order: 'The Fusiliers will spring to attention, fix bayonets and slo-o-o-pe. Taking the word from the Brigadier.' And still at attention he marched away to the farther corner of the bar.

There was nothing secretive about Peter Keary. He stood a little aside from us, and leaned over the counter quizzing the barmaid. In a moment the atmosphere of mystery with which Alec loved to surround himself was dissipated. Peter was small, gay, and quizzical, with a diminutive puckish face and curiously flickering nervous eyelids.

'You're wanted at home, Alec,' he said at last. 'Ginger and I will be up after you.'

Alec obeyed him, and shortly after Peter and I followed. It was a cold gusty night in early spring. Between the public-house and Alec's home there were cottages at each side of the roadway, and, at one side there was a low wall and steps down into a little lane; it was from this that old Kate used to watch on her three-legged stool. The road before us was pitch-black, with only one lamp showing where the steps were. The cottages were white in the darkness, like snow or a very faint moonlight, and our feet started a metallic echo from the flagstones. I spun around when I felt the touch of a hand upon my shoulder, and had almost pulled a gun before I saw who it was.

But it wasn't a soldier, nor a plain-clothes man. It was Najax. Najax, whom I had not spoken to since I was a little boy at school, and she, a girl of seventeen, had been walking out with a colour-sergeant in the British Army. She had obviously been expecting me; her door was open and above the half-door one could see into her little smoky kitchen.

'Larry,' she said shyly, 'I want to speak to you.'

Peter walked stolidly on, and I saw there was nothing else for it but to go in with her. She shut and locked the door behind us. 'Larry,' she said in a low, bitter voice, 'did you hear what happened me?' On the table was a bath in which clothes (the same, I thought, as Alec had kicked about the floor on her) were steeping under a washing board. Najax's arms — fine stout arms they were — were bare to the elbows, and red, having been freshly dried, but I saw that she had been unable to finish her work, that her fury and humiliation had been too much for her. I said something about not minding these things.

'Alec Gorman came in and thrown that bath of water over me. As sure as God is my judge, Larry, he did; and I that never said one unkind word to him. Thrown the water over me and kicked all my nice clean things about the floor.'

'Alec drinks too much,' I said, 'and when he has a drop in there's no answering for what he'll do. But he had no right—'

'And it isn't that I mind so much,' she broke in, 'but he called me — he called me — a spy.' She was scarcely able to bring out the hateful word, and looked up at me with blazing, reckless eyes suffused with tears. 'In my own house he called me a spy. He was put up to that, Larry, he was put up to it, and it was that shameless jade across the way put him up to it, that shameless —'

And this time she was overtaken by tears, real tears, and sat down by the fire, sobbing fiercely with what the people call a *tocht* in her. Then as suddenly she stopped weeping, and tossing the dark hair passionately back from her eyes she looked at me with wild-cat determination.

'I've no one to avenge me, Larry,' she said (she meant her husband, I knew), 'and I'm telling you only because this night I'll go across to that wan and drag her from her bed and crucify her; and I'm telling you, Larry, because I may do her mischief, and you'll know why.'

Her kitchen was bare and dirty; there was a ladder leading up to the loft; a strip of old curtain half hid the bedroom, in which a sacred lamp was burning before a picture of Our Lady of Perpetual Succour and casting a greasy light upon the pillows of the bed. Over the mantelpiece under which we sat was a picture of the Sacred Heart. The tiny window was covered by an old red petticoat, and in the light of an oil lamp bracketed to the wall the white room, with its deal table and bath, its handful of plain chairs, looked hateful and bleak and sordid. And as I became conscious of it I became conscious of an intolerable feeling of pity in myself, that pity which is the curse of our garrulous and emotional race. She was looking up at me, haggard and fierce, and I was aware of the fine modelling of her nose and cheeks, of the hawklike intensity in her, and in a moment I was sitting beside her trying to soothe the wild look out of her eyes.

She was very like a child, and immediately began to cry, softly and without bitterness. I put my hand about her shoulder and began to tease her. My hand slipped from her shoulder to her waist. Suddenly she stopped crying, and taking my free hand in her two damp rough hands, she pulled the fingers this way and that, and told me in a voice half-broken by little sobs that she was no spy; that she had no sympathy with the boys, but wouldn't give one of them away for all the money of Ireland; that she had a cruel life; that she found it hard to be honest when she didn't know at night where tomorrow's dinner would come from.

Often I had seen faces like hers under a street-lamp on the bridge or along the quays. On some bleak and pelting night perhaps such a face would hurry past me, and I would stand for a moment leaning over the parapet, wondering what had driven that terrible look into it, until the face itself would emerge from the blackness of the water below and send me shivering homewards. And so — my arm was about her waist, and when I rose to go she held it there with her hand, so that I had to walk to the door with her in that fashion. I was tempted to kiss her, but my eyes lit upon her long black shawl hanging behind the door and I remembered those faces upon the bridge. Instead of kissing her I made her promise not to fight the old hag opposite, and this she did with the same ready, childish acquiescence.

The night was cold and I ran until I reached the lane where Alec lived. He lived in a sort of lane off a lane, a tiny passage that contained one street lamp and one house. His sister opened to my knock, and going in I saw Alec and Peter at the table behind a barricade of washing. They were having tea, and I sat with them at the rough deal table and drank tea out of a soldier's ponny. The back door was open and Alec's mother was bringing in washing because the skies threatened rain.

I was bombarded with questions about Najax, and then Peter must be told about what happened previously. Peter was sore at it, and with his little face puckered up into a hundred wrinkles he began to remonstrate with Alec, but Alec had almost forgotten the incident and it was only when Peter called it a low-down trick that he began to defend himself. Then his mother (who felt it her bounden duty to join in any remonstrance addressed to Alec) left her work, stood at the foot of the table, and rubbing her hands in her coarse apron and wiping her almost nonexistent nose, said: 'That's right. Speak to him, Mr. Keary, speak to him. And speak to him you, too, Larry. Indeed, it's a shame for him to do a thing like that to a woman that never said a hard word to him, and what will all the neighbours say about us, I'd like to know?'

But Alec told her in a cross voice to shut up for Christ's sake, and Peter realised the futility of saying any more.

After a while Alec and Peter went out into the yard, and through the window I saw them climb over the roof of the jakes into the field beyond. I was left alone with the mother and daughter. The mother was tall and like Alec in appearance, only her nose was phenomenally short and her jaw squarer and slacker. Everything she did was done in exactly the opposite way from Alec's; while every movement of his was vital she worked confusedly and helplessly. She cried frequently and drew her hand across the place where her nose should have been.

'Wisha, Larry,' she said, 'I dunno how 't'll all end, I don't so. And I can't talk to Alec, and I'm sure he'll do something dreadful on me one of these days. I brought him up hard, Larry, and I never grudged him the packet of cigarettes and the bottle of stout, but it'd be dreadful if he was swep' off to his death on me now.'

'Shut up, maa!' her pretty daughter drawled.

'Why should I shut up, child? Sure, he never tells me anything he does except what I hears from the neighbours or what the soldiers tells me when they comes to the house for him. Oh, Larry, it does take the heart out of me when I sees them soldiers walking in with their guns and bayonets and bombs!'

'Oh, shut uuup, maaaa!' the pretty daughter drawled again.

'I won't shut up. Two packages of tea they stole from me the last night they were here, the blackguards, and a pound of cangles! And they tuk the pitcher of Alec in his first knickers, and when I told them how much the knickers cost me the sergeant said "Well, ma'am, if it's any consolation to you, the pair he have on now is the last he'll wear in this world." Oh, *Dhe*! oh, *Dhe*!'

She was sniffling miserably once more, her hands crossed upon her portly bosom when Alec came in carrying two rifles. He looked at her with growing rage.

'Lord. God Almighty, that woman is bawling again!' he shouted. 'Aren't you ever done whinging, huh? ... Ach, go on off ou' that to bed... Take your ma up to bed, Josie!'

'I suppose I'm better,' his mother sniffed. 'Is there anything else you want for the night?'

'There isn't. Did you get me the fags?'

'I did not. Couldn't you have got them yourself below at Miss Mac's?'

'Sure, they won't do me for the night, will they? Josie, run down to the corner shop for two packets of Woodbines.'

'Gi' me the money and I will.'

'Where in the name of God do you think I'd get the money? Here, ma, give Josie the fourpence.'

His mother pulled out a dirty old purse from the pocket of her coarse apron and began to count the money. This was a cause of further sighs. Meantime, Peter had come in and he and I were examining the rifles for rust. And the clack of the bolts and the snapping of the triggers mingled with the clink of money in the old washerwoman's palm and Alec's audacious jests, when another voice joined in; it was the crotchety voice of Alec's father grumbling upstairs about being disturbed.

'Me peace of mind destroyed and me night's rest ruined on me,' he was shouting.

Alec stood at the foot of the stairs and yelled up at him.

'Ah, shut up you! Do you think you're in a mortuary chapel?'

'That's the way he speaks to his own father!' the voice upstairs commented bitterly.

'A lot you have to complain of!' Alec cried gleefully.

'Pity 'tisn't out in the middle of the Sahara you are.'

'Bringing home rifles in the middle of the night when honest men are in bed!'

'Ay, then, and I'm only sorry it isn't a ton of dynamite I have until I'd blow you ou' that bed.'

'Better fed than taught, that's what you are!' the old voice snarled down at us.

'Go on now, go on now!' said Alec with a roar of laughter. 'If you're good, I'll take you out for a nice ride in your pram!'

The grumbling subsided into a moan and the heavy stepping of naked feet on the boards above. But Alec's mother paying homage to a fallen majesty, spoke in a whisper, Josie was sent off for the cigarettes, and the old woman moved on tiptoe to the cupboard and fished out two candles. These she lit and fixed carefully on the table in their own droppings, and still on tiptoe with lips pursed up like a child she quenched the lamp. After a few minutes Josie came back, and the pair of them crept upstairs on their stockinged feet. Peter and I were duly impressed by this dumb show, and for a little while talked in whispers, until some joke of Peter's sent Alec off into a shout of simple mirth; then we pulled our chairs closer up to the table and began to clean and oil the rifles.

II

We seemed to have been hours upon the road; hours, and we were dizzy with fatigue and our fingers clung to the cold rifles. None of us had a watch to measure the time by. We had smoked almost all our cigarettes, and tramped up and down the shelterless country road in the darkness. The night was cold and clear; the wind had dropped, and on the horizon a few, faint stars were burning. Suddenly we heard, dull and far away, a slight boom that seemed to come out of the very heart of the country. We stopped.

'There goes the bridge,' said Alec. 'Thank's be to Christ!'

'Give them a few minutes to get away,' said Peter.

We listened in silence and once again we heard that dull reverberation, only more clearly because we were expecting it.

'You men can say what you like,' said Alec, 'but no barn will see me this night. I'm going where there's a bed waiting for me. Are you game?'

At that moment there were few things we should not have been game for. We followed him across the fields to a quiet suburban road on which there were a bare half-dozen houses, houses of the well-to-do people. Here among a mass of disused stables we tried to find a hidingplace in which to leave our rifles for the night. At last Alec hit upon the idea of putting them down a chimney-stack. If we had not been so confoundedly sleepy neither Peter nor I would have listened to him, but, because we were, he got his way.

Taking a ladder and a piece of rope he climbed on to the roof of the stables. I handed him up the rifles and he tied them together, dropped them down the chimney-stack — the fireplace, by the way, had been built across — and secured the rope to a nail inside. It was only after we had cleared away the ladder again that it struck him there was no protection for the rifles if rain came on, but by this time we shouldn't have minded throwing them into the river to get rid of them.

It was beautiful up there where we were. The whole valley of the river was spread out beneath us. The river itself, fringed by a few street-lamps, glowed here and there, and on its bank a factory and a railway station were busily lighted. Further off was the city, distinguishable by its massed lights that outlined on either side the two great hills flanking it. One could pick out certain familiar spots on the hills by the line that the winding street-lamps made. As we turned up the avenue towards the house a dog began to bark; another answered him, and in a moment the whole place was a riot of yelping dogs; the barking came to us like an echo from very far away, and it seemed as if even in the city the damned brutes scented our approach. For the first time that night I was nervous, and tugged with all my might at the old house-bell. It pealed through the silent rooms within and wakened yet another dog who added his voice to the chorus. There was no other answer and we tugged again and again. At last we heard the pattering of bare feet in the hall. The door opened an inch or two and we pushed it in, on top of an old man who, with one hand, was holding up the breeches that sagged about his toes. I switched an electric torch in his face for a moment, a bleak, wintry, old face it was, the flesh converging in deep hollows to the unshaven chin, a toothless, snarling mouth and above it two sleepy, cold, blue eyes.

'We want a bed for the night, neighbour,' said Alec.

'There's many wants beds that can't afford them. Who are ye?'

'Never mind. Any place will do us. I suppose we're late or supper.'

'Is it the hunt is after ye?'

'Never mind, I say,' Alec exploded losing his temper.

'All right, all right.'

'One good bed is all we ask. The master is away?'

'He is away.'

'A sound judge, the master! There are a few things we'd like to say to him if he came back.'

The old man showed us into a long low room lined with bookshelves. There were two beds in it, and with a sigh of relief Alec threw his cap on the dressing-table and began to unpin his collar.

'Ye'll be quiet now?'

'We'll be quiet, neighbour, don't you fret. You go and have a good sleep. And try to forget there did anyone call because we'd leave more than a wife and children to regret us.'

Old Rip Van Winkle pattered away. Alec having removed his tie and collar and boots, went heavily on his knees, and Peter after a little while did the same. Peter's prayers were short, and before sleep overcame me, he was lying beside me in the bed; but my eyes closed on Alec's devotions, and I remember him foggily with his eyes turned up to Heaven, beating his breast and mumbling fervent ejaculations.

When I woke it was morning and Peter had gone. I glanced around me; saw that Alec was asleep, and noticed with satisfaction the three revolvers lying on the little table between his bed and mine. I dozed again and awoke slowly with an extraordinary feeling of oppression. The room was as still as before, but it was much colder, and as I opened my eyes I found myself staring blankly into the face of a man in civilian clothes who was sitting on the end of my bed, smoking a cigarette. Then I noticed that this strange man was holding a service revolver upon his knee, and a sick feeling of hysteria began to penetrate deep into my bowels. I turned my head cautiously and saw Alec sitting up in bed very wakeful, the clothes drawn tight about him. The room was full of men; I took them in one by one only to realise that I was lying on the bed with nothing but a singlet on.

'Well?' asked the man with the gun, and I could only grin vacantly. Then I remembered the three revolvers and realised that we would face the firing squad because of them. On the instant I was broad awake. I looked at the little table — the revolvers were gone! As if all too clearly reading what had been in my mind the man with the gun —rapped out:

'Now, where's that gun of yours, Ginger?'

'Bloody well you know he have no gun.' Alec had rapped out the reply before I could speak.

'Oh, no, he haven't,' the other said mockingly. 'Well, Ginger ?'

'I haven't a gun,' I said, taking my cue from Alec. A titter went round the room. But for the life of me I could not guess what had happened to the revolvers, and for a moment a delicious sensation of relief went through my body; but only for a moment, and again the misery of a trapped creature sank deep into my bowels.

'Get up!' one of the men ordered, and Alec and I got up and dressed. Meanwhile, the soldiers pulled drawers and bedclothes about in the search for arms, for arms that miraculously were not there. Then we marched down to the waiting lorries through lines of laurel and laburnum. There were more soldiers outside and we were greeted with cheers and jibes. An officer struck Alec on the side of the face with his clenched fist. These were only the details: as were the drive through quiet suburbs and early-morning streets, the clerks and shopgirls going to their work, the girl I recognised upon the pathway and in whom I said good-bye to everything I held dear — and how much dearer now — houses and people and things, home and work and pleasure, freedom certainly, perhaps life.

We were at the courthouse. We went up the steps; the clerks were turning in by ones and twos and looked at us curiously. We were taken downstairs and left in a filthy underground cell where five or six other men sat up and stared at us. Conversation was impossible, for one of the group was almost certain to be a spy. About an hour later Alec and I were called out together into the dark corridor and two or three officers set upon us.

'Where are the bombs, Ginger?'

'Now, Gorman, you'd better say where the dump is.'

'We have no dump,' Alec said sullenly.

'No dump? No dump? Where are the three skits you had last night in Norton's?'

'We had no skits.'

'Oh no. And you had nothing to do with the bridges or the trapmine either? Mr. Peter Keary has told us about that already. Now, out with it if you want to save your skin!'

Peter? So Peter was caught too!

'If he told you all that why didn't he tell you the rest?' Alec snarled.

In an instant he was grovelling upon the ground with a blow from a revolver butt, and one of the inquisitors kicked him in the stomach.

'None of your backchat. You're for it. D'ye hear me? You'll get yours. Now where are those guns?'

Alec began to groan and the groan rose to a squeal as the officer kicked him again. The officer shouted at him to be quiet, but Alec only screamed louder, like a man who was in mortal pain; then I said something wild — I don't remember what it was — and found myself being throttled while somebody hammered my head against the wall. It was all pitiably dark, and I could only see the shadow of the man who was throttling me.

We were chucked back into the cell, I without a collar and with the neck torn from my shirt; Alec whining and holding his stomach. When we got inside I put my hand on his shoulder and said something; he continued whining and I was astonished at his softness. He threw himself upon a mattress in a corner, his knees doubled up to his stomach, and lay there, silent but for an occasional groan, until we were called out again. Then I began to get worried for him, because he had to be helped out of the cell and back but if it served no other purpose it saved us from anything more serious than a chucking about and another throttling for me. That went on for the best part of the day; in the evening I saw a friendly face among the officers outside; an officer that had been in our battalion at one time, and succeeded in getting him to order our removal to the prison.

An hour later the prison gate closed behind us. As we walked in darkness up the old garden path and through the Governor's office into one of the halls of the prison I felt in my soul it was for good. At first I stood stupefied in the great circular pit, lit by hissing blue and yellow gasflares that flickered wildly in the breeze blowing through four barred gateways. An iron staircase up to an iron balcony with high barred windows and a circle of white faces; above that another balcony and more faces peering down at us through the half-darkness, that was what I saw. A Dantesque vision. The flags under my feet were islanded by pools of rain-water, and in spite of the wind there was a stink of refuse and humanity.

From the balconies, each with its four great barred windows, long corridors of cells went off into the three wings of the prison. Alec and I were put into a tiny cell lit by a single gasflare; a cell scarcely big enough for one man, with an unglazed window next the ceiling. A man was sitting upon the floor hammering at a piece of bright metal on a metal rod. He was making a ring for his girl, he said, and it was a shilling piece which he had impaled upon the rod. After a while he got up and made tea for us in a dixie which he hung over the gasflare. Then we all went out on to the balcony for the saying of the rosary, and after that lay down upon two mattresses stretched upon the floor and covered ourselves with a few blankets. When the three of us were lying close together we completely filled the available floor space though another mattress had to be left upon the waterpipes for a fourth man. After a time Alec began to shiver and complain again; he couldn't sleep, he said, and was very ill with the pain in his stomach. He went along the corridor to the latrine and got sick before he reached it. The other man, who was an ex-soldier, then insisted upon sitting up, striking a match, and showing us the wound he had received during the great war

'You've nothing wrong with you as bad as that,' he said angrily to Alec.

'Look at me! Feel my ribs! Feel my ribs! There isn't as much as a pick of flesh on my bones from it!'

'Why don't you talk to the doctor?' I asked.

'He says I'm shamming, the blackguard!' said the ex-soldier settling down again with a groan.

I fell into a half sleep while the men on either side of me turned and twisted and sighed; when I woke it was to see a lantern shining upon me on the floor. It was the officer of the watch staging another capture — this time it was Peter. I sprang up and lit the gas. Peter wore no collar and his face was deathly pale. He sat down on the waterpipes with his head between his hands; then he took off his cap and I saw that he was wearing about his head a bandage, stained with blood. He was trembling all over and did not speak.

The sentry below bawled out to quench the light and I did so. Only then did Peter tell us what had happened to him. He had been captured by a second party of soldiers on his way in; they had taken him with them to where our fellows had laid a trapmine the previous night and tried to make him dig it up. But Peter had been fly and refused to dig; then they tried to make him run with the intention of shooting him as an escaping prisoner.

He had refused to run and, in a rage, one of them had fired, wounding him slightly in the head. As he still stood his ground they brought him back, and that night, after we had left, hell had broken loose in the Courthouse. They had taken one man to the top of a flight of stairs; flung him down; prodded him with bayonets, and kicked him about the floor. Peter did not say much but we had good reason to know what he meant. Then, suddenly, Alec began to moan and shiver again, and I made Peter and the other keep still.

Next morning, to my great surprise, Alec woke in what, even for him, was high spirits. He went about the prison, chatting with everyone he knew and laughing boisterously. It was only after a while that I got him alone. He told me that on the previous morning he had pushed the revolvers in behind a shelf of books just as the soldiers were coming in the hallway. This gave me a fresh start.

If the old man had really given us away, as Alec suspected, he must find the revolvers sooner or later and perhaps send us before a court-martial. But it was no use telling Alec anything of that kind then. He was full of plans for an escape of all the prisoners. He had made them up during the night. We were to dig a tunnel or fight our way through the guard. It was perfectly simple, perfectly simple to himself. And it was only towards evening that the older hands succeeded in persuading him that one idea was as impossible as the other. Then he returned to the cell, looking wan and distraught, began to complain again of pains and lay on the floor for hours without speaking.

Next day he looked so ill we called in the prison doctor. The doctor left some iodine and "black jack" (the only medicine he was ever known to administer). That day there were several rows between Alec and the original occupant of the cell, who was angry that the doctor had paid attention to Alec, and insisted on hammering at his silly old ring in the cell. He kept on mumbling indignantly to himself about shamming and malingering until at last Alec, in a towering rage, caught him in his two powerful arms, carried him out to the corridor, and swung him over the balcony rail, threatening to toss him into the suicide net. After this the ex-soldier refused to speak to any of us again.

Within four or five days I was shocked at the appearance of Alec. He looked like a man in galloping consumption. His cheeks had fallen in, he could not bring himself to eat, and now and again he rose and tramped fiercely up and down the corridor alone. When Peter and I approached him he looked at us blankly, as though he did not recognise us. Then he answered offhand and resumed his tortured walking. Every muscle in his face seemed to be drawn tight, and there was a glint of insanity in his eyes. Several times each night he woke us with his muffled shouting and groaning, and his powerful limbs tossed this way and that, in the grip of his dreams.

Another thing I noticed. He came to be too friendly with the officer of the watch, and after the count each evening, he spoke to him, sometimes in the cell, sometimes apart in the corridor. His overtures were marked; there was a whine in his voice, and he protested too much about his innocence. It was the officer of the watch who suggested to him that he should sign a declaration of allegiance, and, after a night of indecision that was a torture to Peter and me, Alec agreed. He signed, but that was all that came of it; those outside knew whom they had to deal with as well as we, and Alec remained a prisoner.

Then one evening, without a word to either of us, he disappeared with the officer of the watch. It raised no comment at the time, because men were frequently taken out to be questioned in that way, but Peter and I smiled at one another and shrugged our shoulders. We knew that Alec had agreed to show some of our hiding-places to the soldiers. And when an hour passed and Alec did not return we had to endure the questions of scores of men who hung about our cell, coming in, going out, passing a sly remark, and nodding their heads grimly. It was only when the ex-soldier, looking up from his ring-making, came out with the ugly word that was in all our minds that Peter lost his temper, and after that the squabble between them diverted us until midnight.

All next day we sat in misery, and the next, and the next. Then because in prison no mood can last for long without bringing disaster we both began to cheer up. I think the cause of the good humour on my part was a parcel I received early in the morning of the fourth day; it contained only a big wheelcake and a note. 'Dear Larry,' the note ran, 'I enclose a cake which I made specialy for you. I hope you will like it. Your poor mother is looking very well but she is looking very sad poor woman. I was glad to see One You Know at home again and he appolijised. He said you were speaking to him about me as well as Mr. Keary for which I am truly grateful. I hope in God to see you home again soon. —Yours truly, Norah Gillespie. X X X X X.'

It was the first news we had received of Alec, and though it confirmed our worst suspicions, we were not angry with him. We were curious only to know what he had done or said to get himself out. We did not even blame him; we loved him too much for that, and in our hearts we know that he had done the only thing it was in his nature to do.

But this thinking of him, seeing him visit Najax and stand at the bar to drink his pint with the rest, stimulated our curiosity; not only did we want to know how he had bought his release; we wanted to hear him explain it all word for word, to the neighbours, to old Kate, to Najax to Mike and his companions — as we knew he would. In a way we were happy, as happy as we could be with those three revolvers lying behind a row of books in Norton's house, for these, as often as we thought of them, chilled us again. And that evening, as though to satisfy our curiosity, a fresh batch of prisoners arrived; amongst them a poor innocent from our own locality, a suspect. We fell on him together with our questions.

He looked at us in stupefaction. 'Didn't ye hear?' he asked, and we were too wild with him to answer.

'Sure, God Almighty,' he cried, 'the whole world know of it by now. How he took them out some place there was rifles hid? In a chimney?'

'Yes, yes,' said Peter and I together.

'And went up on the roof with them to show them there was no trap. And flung two of them head and neck back into the yard, and jumped clear off at the other side into a lot of bushes and brambles.'

'Alec,' said Peter, 'our Alec. He did? He got away from them?'

'Of course he got away. He jumped from the roof in the darkness.' The poor innocent raised his voice until it pealed through the corridor and brought out head after head to inquire what was up. "The grandest, the most desperate, the most magnificent escape ever made. He have a charmed life. Didn't I see him with my own two eyes swaggering about the cross yesterday with a gun in his breeches pocket? Didn't I? Didn't I see him drinking at Miss Mac's, and visiting the neighbours? Didn't I? More than poor devils like us can do without being caught. He have a charmed life I tell you!'

Visiting the neighbours! How like him it was, our own inimitable Alec. Then Peter held out his hand to me.

'We're safe,' he said in a low voice. 'We're safe,' said I.

'And whisper," said the innocent, putting his arms round both our shoulders and winking solemnly to right and left. 'I'll tell you something I wouldn't tell the others. Between you and me Alec is at his old tricks again.'

'How so?' we asked.

'How so? Look here to me!' He pulled out a dirty copy of the newspaper for the previous day. 'Read that and tell me in confidence what you think of it.' He pointed to a short paragraph at the foot of one page.

'Dunmerial, the beautiful suburban residence of Mr Edmund Norton, was burned to the ground in the early hours of this morning by a party of men, wearing masks and carrying petrol tins and revolvers. The caretaker, Michael Horgan, an old man, is in hospital, suffering from exposure and injuries said to be the result of a beating. He is not expected to recover.'

'There!' said the innocent with a triumphant glance, 'there now! "He is not expected to recover?" What do you make of that?'

Day Dreams

Except for occasional moments of embarrassment I never really minded being out of work. I lived at home, so I didn't need money, and though this made things harder for Mother, and Father put on a sour puss about having to feed and clothe me, I spent so much of my time out of doors that I didn't need to think about them. The uncomfortable moments came when I saw some girl I knew on a tram and could not get on it because I could not pay her fare, or when I was walking with some fellows whose conversation I enjoyed and I had to make some excuse to leave them when they went in for a drink. At times like these I was very sorry for myself and very angry with people and life.

Never for long though, and the rest of the time I was perfectly happy, for I was free to go on with my own thoughts. I wasn't opposed to work on principle because I knew a number of quite nice people who thought highly of it, but I did think that in practice people wasted too much valuable time on it for the little it gave them back. Most of the time I had worked on the railway I had been miserable, doing things I disliked and talking to chaps to whom I felt indifferent.

When the weather was really too bad I sat in the reading-room in the public library and read steadily through all the reviews and periodicals, about the crisis in British politics, penal reform, unemployment and social security. I was very strongly in favour of social security. When the weather was fair, and even when it wasn't, I walked a great deal; and because I felt I really had no right to my walks, they gave me something of the same pleasure I felt as a kid when I went on the lang from school. There is only one element common to all forms of romance guilt, and I felt guilty about my views on the Conservative Party and social security, while all the places I walked in had a curious poetic aura, as though each of them belonged to an entirely different country; the Glen to Scotland, the country north of our house, with its streams and fields and neat little farmhouses, to England, the river-roads to the Rhineland; so that it would not have surprised me in the least if the people I met in them all spoke different languages.

Each neighbourhood, too, had its own sort of imaginary girl; noble and tragic in the Glen, gentle and charming in the English countryside, subtle and cultivated along the river, like the big houses that stood there, sheltered behind their high stone walls. Sometimes we just met and talked since she shared my liking for the countryside; and we both realised as we told one another the story of our lives, that, different in most ways as these were, we had everything else in common. She was usually rich English or American; and I had to persuade her about the political folly of her class, but this never seemed to offer any difficulties to her clear and sympathetic intelligence.

But at other times, perhaps when the feeling of guilt was strongest in me, she would be in some serious difficulty; being run away with by a wild horse, flying from kidnappers or just drowning. At the right moment with a coolness that was bound to appeal to any girl I stepped in; stopped the horse, scattered the gangsters or swam ashore with her from the sinking boat. Though modesty required that I should then leave without telling her my name, leaving her to a lifelong search, it nearly always happened that I accompanied her back to the Imperial Hotel and was introduced to her father who was naturally grateful and besides, had been looking for a young man just like me with a real understanding of the political situation to take over his business. If I thought of my own position at all on those walks it was only with a gentle regret that economic conditions deprived the world of the attention of a really superior mind. And the worse my situation was, the better my mind functioned.

My real difficulty came from good-natured friends who didn't, as they would have put it, want to see me wasting my time. They were always trying to get me introductions to influential people who might be able to fit me in somewhere as a warehouse clerk at thirty bob a week. I knew they meant it well, and I did my best to be grateful, but they hurt me more than Father did with his scowling and snarling, or any of the handful of enemies I had in the locality who, I knew, talked of me as a good-for nothing or a half-idiot. 'Well, Larry,' my friends would say sagaciously, 'you're getting on, you know. 'Twon't be long now till you're twenty, and even if it was only a small job, it would be better than nothing.' And I would look at them sadly and realise that they were measuring me up against whatever miserable sort of vacancy they were capable of imagining, and seeing no disparity between us. Of course I interviewed the influential people they sent me to, and pretended a lifelong interest in double-entry book-keeping though I never had been able to understand the damned thing, and tried to look like a quiet, hard-working, religious boy who would never give any trouble. I could scarcely tell the owner of a big store that I liked being out of work. Anyway, I doubt if there was any need, because any jobs they had didn't come my way. One night I went all the way to Blackrock, a little fishing village down the river from Cork, to see a solicitor who was supposed to have an interest in some new factory, and he talked to me for two solid hours about the commercial development of the city, and at the end of it all said he'd keep me in mind in case anything turned up. I left his house rather late and discovered to my disgust that I hadn't the price of the tram. This was one of my really bad moments. To feel guilty and have to walk is one thing; to feel as virtuous as I did after talking for hours about reclamation schemes and still have to walk is another. Besides, I had no cigarettes.

There were two ways into town; one through the suburbs, the other a little shorter, along the riverbank, and I chose this. It was a pleasant enough place by day; a river-walk called the Marina facing a beautiful road called Tivoli at the other side, and above Tivoli were the sandstone cliffs and expensive villas of Montenotte, all named with the nostalgia of an earlier day. It had an avenue of trees, a bandstand, seats for the nursemaids and two guns captured in the Crimea over which the children climbed. It was part of the Rhineland of my day dreams, but by night the resemblance was not so clear. As it approached the city it petered out in jetties, old warehouses and badly lit streets of sailors' lodging-houses.

I had just emerged into this part when I heard a woman scream. It startled me out of my reverie, and I stood and looked about me. It was very dark. Then under a gas lamp at the corner of a warehouse I saw a man and a woman in some sort of cling. The woman was screaming her head off, and, thinking that she might have been taken ill, I ran towards them. As I did, the man broke away and walked quickly up the quay, and the woman stopped screaming and began to sob, turning her face to the wall in a curiously childish gesture of despair. As she wasn't sick, I felt awkward and merely stopped and raised my cap.

'Can I help you, miss?' I asked doubtfully. She shook her head several times without looking at me.

'The dirty rat!' she sobbed, rubbing her face with her hand, and then she poured forth a stream of language I had never heard the like of and some of which I didn't understand at all. 'All I earned the last two nights he took from me, the rat! the rat!'

'But why did he do that?' I asked, wondering if the man could be her husband, and she gaped at me in astonishment, the tears still streaming down her little painted face. It wouldn't have been a bad face if only she'd let it alone.

'Because he says 'tis his beat,' she said. 'All the girls has to pay him. He says 'tis for protection.'

'But why don't you tell the police?' I asked.

'The police?' she echoed in the same tone. 'A hell of a lot the police care about the likes of us. Only to get more out of us, if they could.'

'But how much did he take?' I asked.

'Five quid,' she replied, and began to sob again, taking out a dirty little handkerchief to dab her eyes. 'Five blooming quid! All I earned in the past two nights! And now there won't be another ship for a week, and the old landlady will be after me for the rent.'

'All right,' I said, coming to a quick decision, 'I'll ask him about it.'

Which was exactly as far as I proposed to go. It was all still well beyond my comprehension. I quickened my step and went after the footsteps I heard retreating up the quay. Like all dreamy and timid people who will do anything to avoid a row on their own account, I have always taken an unnatural delight in those that other people thrust on me. It never even crossed my mind that I was in a dangerous locality and that I might quite well end up in the river with a knife in my back.

Some of my doubts were dispelled when the man in front of me looked back and began to run. This seemed like an admission of guilt so I ran too. Since I walked miles every day I was in excellent condition, and I knew he had small chance of getting away from me. He soon realised this as well and stopped with his back to the wall of a house and his right arm lifted. He was a tall, thin fellow with a long, pasty, cadaverous face, a moustache that looked as though it had been put in with an eyebrow pencil, and sideburns. He was good-looking too in his own coarse way.

'Excuse me,' I said, panting but still polite, 'the lady behind seems to think you have some money of hers.'

'Lady?' he snarled. 'What lady? That's no lady, you fool!'

I didn't like his tone and I strongly resented his words. I realised now what the girl behind me was but that made no difference to me. I had been brought up to treat every woman as a lady, and had no idea that a crook is as sensitive about respectability as a bank manager. It really pains him to have to deal with immoral women.

'I didn't know,' I said apologetically. 'I'm sorry. But I promised to ask you about the money.'

'Ask what you like!' he said, beginning to shout. 'The money is mine.'

'Oh, you mean she took it from you?' I said, thinking I was beginning to see the truth at last.

'Who said she took it from me?' he growled, as though I had accused him of something really bad. 'She owes it to me.'

Apparently I wasn't really seeing daylight.

'You mean you lent it to her?' I asked, but that only seemed to make him mad entirely.

'What the hell do you think I am?' he asked arrogantly. 'A money-lender? She agreed to pay me to look after her, and now she's trying to rob me.'

'But how do you look after her?' I asked quite innocently as it happened though he didn't seem to think so.

'How do I look after her?' he repeated. 'My God, man, a woman would have no chance in a place like this without a man to look after her. Or have you any idea what it's like?'

I hadn't, and I regretted it. It struck me that perhaps I wasn't really justified in interfering; that people had their own arrangements and she might have tried some sharp practice on him. I did not realise that every crook has to have a principle to defend; otherwise, he would be compelled to have a low opinion of himself which is something that no crook likes. It was the fellow's manner I distrusted. If only he had been polite I wouldn't have dreamed of interfering.

'But in that case, surely you should let her look after herself,' I said.

'What the hell do you mean?'

'I mean, if she broke a bargain, you should just refuse to look after her any more,' I explained reasonably. 'That ought to bring her to her senses, and if it doesn't, anything that happens is her own fault.'

He looked at me incredulously as though I was an idiot, which, recollecting the whole incident is about the only way I can describe myself.

'If I were you,' I went on, 'I'd simply give her back the money and have nothing more to do with her.'

'I'll do nothing of the sort,' he said, drawing himself up. 'That money is mine. I told you that.'

'Now, look,' I said almost pleadingly, 'I don't want to have a row with you about it. It's only the state she's in.'

'You think you can make me?' he asked threateningly.

'Well, I promised the girl,' I said.

I know it sounds feeble, but feeble was what my position was, not knowing right from wrong in the matter. He glanced up the quay, and for a moment I thought he was going to make a bolt for it, but he decided against it. God knows why! I can't have looked very formidable. Then he drew himself up to his full height, the very picture of outraged rectitude, gave me a couple of pound notes, turned on his heel and began to walk away. I counted the notes and suddenly became absolutely furious. 'Come back here, you!' I said.

'What the hell is it now?' he asked as though this was the last indignity.

'I want the rest of that money,' I said.

'That's all she give me,' he snarled. 'What's this? A holdup?'

'That's what it's going to be unless you hand over what you stole, God blast you!' I said. Now no further doubts contained the flood of indignation that was rising in me. I had given him every opportunity of explaining himself and behaving like a gentleman, and this was how he had repaid me. I knew that a man who had tried to deceive me at such a moment was only too capable of deceiving a defenceless girl, and I was determined that he should deceive her no longer. He gave me the money, a bit frightened in his manner, and I added bitingly: 'And next time you interfere with that girl, you'd better know what's going to happen you. For two pins I'd pitch you in the river, sideburns and all, you dirty, lying little brute!'

It alarms me now to write of my own imprudence, but even that did not rouse him to fighting, and he went off up the quay, muttering to himself. The girl had crept nearer us as we argued and now she rushed up to me, still weeping.

'God bless you, boy, God bless you!' she said wildly. 'I'll pray for you the longest day I live, for what you done for me.'

And then suddenly I felt very weak, and realised that I was trembling all over, trembling so that I could scarcely move. Heroism, it seemed, did not come naturally to me. All the same I managed to muster up a smile.

'You'd better let me see you home,' I said. 'I don't think you'll have any more trouble with that fellow, but just at the moment it might be better not to meet him alone.'

'Here,' she said, giving me back two of the five notes I had handed her. 'Take these. For yourself !'

'I will not, indeed,' I said, laughing. 'For what?'

'That's all you know, boy,' she said bitterly. 'That fellow have the heart scalded out of the poor unfortunate girls here. A hard life enough they have without it, the dear God knows!'

'If he talks to you again, tell him you'll put me on him,' I said. 'Delaney is my name. Larry Delaney. Tell him I'm a middle-weight champion. I'm not, but he won't know.' And I laughed again, in sheer relief.

'Go on, Larry!' she said determinedly, trying to make me take the two banknotes. 'Take them!'

'I'll do nothing of the sort,' I said. 'But I'll take a fag if you have one. I'm dying for a hale.'

'God, isn't it the likes of you would be without them?' she said, fumbling in her bag. 'Here, take the packet, boy! I have tons.'

'No, thanks,' I said. 'It's just that I get a bit excited.' Which was a mild way of describing the way my hands jumped when I stood and tried to light that cigarette. She saw it too.

'What brought you down here at all?' she asked inquisitively.

'I had to walk from Blackrock,' I said.

'And where do you work? Or are you still at school?'

'I'm not working at the moment,' I said. 'That's what took me out to Blackrock, looking for a job.'

'God help us, isn't it hard?' she said. 'But you won't be long that way with God's help. You have the stuff in you, Larry, not like most of them. You're only a boy, but you stood up to that fellow that was twice your age.'

'Oh, him!' I said with a sniff. 'He's only a blow-hole.'

'Them are the dangerous ones, boy,' she said shrewdly with a queer trick she had of narrowing her eyes. 'Them are the ones you'd have to mind, or a bit of lead piping on the back of your head is what you'd be getting when you weren't looking.'

Frightened by her own words, she stopped and looked behind her. 'Look, like a good boy,' she went on eagerly, 'take the old couple of quid! Go on! Ah, do, can't you! Sure, you're out of a job don't I know damn well what 'tis like? I suppose you had to walk from Blackrock because you hadn't the price of the tram. Do, Larry boy! Do! Just for fags! From me!'

She stuffed the money into the pocket of my jacket, and I suddenly found that I wanted it. Not only for its own sake, though it meant riches to me, but because she was that sort of woman; warm and generous and addle-pated and because I knew it would give her a feeling of satisfaction. Because I was in an excited, emotional state, her emotion infected me. All the same I put a good face on it.

'That's all right,' I said. 'I'll borrow it, and be very grateful. But I'm going to pay it back. And I don't know your name or where you live.'

'Ah, for God's sake!' she exclaimed with a joyous laugh. 'Forget about it! So long as I have enough to keep the old landlady's puss off me. But if you want to see me, my name is Molly Leahy, and I have a room here. But they all know me. You have only to ask for me.'

We shook hands and I promised to see her soon again. Mind, I meant that. I went over the bridges in a halo of self-satisfaction. I felt I had had a great adventure, had added a whole new area to my experience, and had learned things about life that nobody could ever have taught me.

That mood of exaltation lasted just as long as it took me to reach the well-lit corner by the cinema in King Street, and then it disappeared, and I stood there in a cold wind, unable to face the thought of returning home. I knew the reason without having to examine my conscience. It was the damned money in my pocket. It had nothing to do with the girl, or how she had earned it; nothing even to do with the fact that she needed it a great deal more than I did and probably deserved it more. It was just that I realised that the great moment of my day dreams had come to me without my recognising it; that I had behaved myself as I had always hoped I would behave, and I had then taken pay for it and in this world need never expect more. Someone passed and looked back at me curiously, and I realised that I had been talking to myself.

Outside the Scots Church at the foot of Summerhill an old woman in a shawl was sitting on the low wall with her bag by her side.

'Gimme a few coppers for the night, sir, and that the Almighty God may make your bed in heaven,' she whined.

'Here you are, ma'am,' I said with a laugh, handing her the two pound notes.

Then I hurried up the hill, pursued by her clamour. Of course, the moment I had done it, I knew it was wrong; the exhibitionist behaviour of someone who was trying to reconcile the conflict in himself by a lying dramatic gesture. Next day I would be without cigarettes again and cursing myself for a fool. I was really destitute now, without money or self-respect.

After that I could find no pleasure in my solitary walks; the imaginary girls were all gone. I took the first job I was offered, but by the time I had saved two pounds and started to look down the Marina for Molly Leahy, she had disappeared; I suppose to Liverpool or Glasgow or one of the other safety-valves by which we pious folk keep ourselves safe in our own day dreams.